DEADLY LITTLE SECRET

Also by Laurie Faria Stolarz

DEADLY LITTLE SECRET

A **TOUCH** NOVEL

Laurie Faria Stolarz

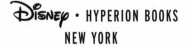 · HYPERION BOOKS
NEW YORK

For my mother,
who gave me the creativity to write,
and for MaryKay,
who showed me I could

I

I COULD HAVE DIED THREE MONTHS AGO.

Ever since, things haven't quite been the same for me.

It happened on the last day of school. I was walking across the parking lot by the gym when my earring slipped off—a hammered sterling-silver hoop with a clasp that never seemed to fit quite right. But the pair was my favorite, given to me by my mother just months before, on my sixteenth birthday.

I squatted down to search the pavement. Everything that happened next sped by in what felt like a three-second blur: Gloria Beckham's car peeling across the parking lot in my direction. Me, sort of frozen there, on hands and knees, assuming the car would come to a sudden halt when she saw me.

It didn't.

It kept racing toward me, toward the two hockey nets

that Todd McCaffrey had left in the middle of the lot while he went in to fetch more equipment. At some point, I heard Todd's voice yell out, "Stop!" Then the car plowed into the hockey nets at a speed high enough to crush them beneath the grill.

And it didn't stop there. The car continued toward me without missing a beat.

I imagine that my heart sped up, that my adrenaline did that hormonal-pumping thing it does when it's trying to brace you for what happens next. But what happened next I could never have prepared myself for.

Being shoved out of the way.

My shoulders slamming against the curb with enough force to cover my back in bruises and scabs for the next several weeks.

The burning of my skin as my shirt lifted up and the small of my back scraped against the pavement, tearing off two layers of skin.

And the peculiar way he touched me.

"Are you okay?" the mystery boy asked.

I opened my mouth to say something—to ask him what happened, to see about Gloria, to find out who he was.

But then: "Shhh . . . don't try and talk," he whispered.

The truth is I *couldn't* talk. It felt like my chest had broken open, like someone had cracked me in two and stolen my breath.

"Blink once if you're okay," he continued, "twice if you need to go to the hospital."

I blinked once, but I honestly didn't want to. I didn't want to stop looking at him for even one solitary moment—the sharp angles of his face; his dark gray eyes, flecked with gold; and those pale pink lips pressed together with concern—despite how inappropriate the moment was for gawking.

He glanced over his shoulder in search of Todd, who had gone to help Gloria.

"I called nine-one-one!" Todd shouted out.

The boy, probably a year or two older than I was, turned his focus back to me. His shoulders, broad and strong under his navy blue T-shirt, hovered right above my chest. "Are you sure you're going to be okay?" His face was so close I could smell his skin—a mixture of sugar and sweat.

I nodded and let out a breath, relieved that my lungs were still working. "How's Gloria?" I mouthed; no sound came out.

He looked toward her car again. It had finally come to a stop halfway up the grassy hill that ran along the side of the school.

The boy, noticing our closeness maybe, sat back on his heels then and ran his fingers through his perfectly rumpled dark hair.

And then he touched me.

His hand rested on my stomach, almost by accident I think, because the gesture seemed to startle him even more than it startled me. He stared at me with new intensity, his eyes wide and urgent, his lips slightly parted.

"What is it?" I asked, noticing the scar on his forearm—a narrow gash that branched off in two directions, like a broken tree limb.

Instead of answering, he pressed his palm harder against me and closed his eyes. His wrist grazed the bare skin right above my navel, where my sweater was still pulled up.

It nearly made me lose my breath all over again.

A moment later an ambulance came zooming into the lot, the siren blaring, the lights flashing bright red and white, and the boy backed away, just like that.

He crawled free of me, darted over to his motorcycle. Hopped on. Revved up the engine. And then sped away.

Before I could even ask him his name.

Before I could thank him for saving my life.

2

The first time I saw her I knew—long and twisty caramel-blond hair, curvy hips, and lips the color of fire.

She was talking that first time—in a group of faceless girls. I was there, too—standing a good distance back. Watching her.

I wondered what she was all about—if her cheeks were naturally seashell pink, or if she was embarrassed or maybe wearing makeup.

I watched her lips as they pouted, then stretched wide when she laughed. It made me laugh, too. I couldn't stop watching her, imagining the way her mouth would move when she said my name, or told me she loved me, or came at me with a kiss.

And so, I made a silent vow to myself that day. I would find out about her cheeks, and the way her kisses would taste. I would find out everything, because I simply had to know. I had to have her. I still do. And one day, very soon, I will.

3

It's BEEN THREE MONTHS since the accident, and while my burns, blisters, and bruises have all healed, there's a piece that still feels broken. And, no, it's not my heart or anything sentimental like that. I'm not one of those overly emotional damsels in distress, eagerly awaiting her prince to come and save her. A little closure, please, is all I ask—the opportunity to see that boy just one more time—to tell him "thank you," to ask him what he was doing there in the first place.

And to find out why he touched me like that.

"A little frustrated, are we?" Kimmie asks, noticing the oomph with which I wedge out my clay.

It's C-Block pottery class, and I'm working the air pockets from my mound of sticky redness by thwacking, plopping, and kneading it against the table.

"Personally, I'm surprised you haven't cracked completely," she continues.

"Don't you have some clay to wedge?" I ask her.

"Don't you have some life to get?"

I ignore her comment and proceed to remind her that unwedged clay means a sculpture that's bound to be blown to bits in the kiln.

"Maybe I like bits."

"Do you like slime? Because that's what your piece is starting to look like." I pass her a sponge for the excess water.

"Honestly, Camelia, your control-freakish ways are starting to get a little old. You really *should* get out more."

Kimmie and I have been friends since kindergarten—through who-can-blow-the-bigger-Hubba-Bubba-bubble-gum contests to the time in the eighth grade when Jim Konarski spun the bottle and I had to kiss him. For the record, I still get crap about missing his lips entirely and accidentally tonguing his left nostril.

"I'm fine," I assure her.

She takes a moment to look me over—from my unruly dirty-blond locks and giraffelike neck to my self-declared lack of style. Today: a long-sleeved T, dark-washed jeans, and a pair of black ballet flats—exactly what the mannequin at the Gap was wearing.

"Fine?" she says, working her mound of clay into what appears to be an anatomically correct man: pecs, package, and all. "Miss I Spend My Saturday Nights Playing Makeover with My Nine-Year-Old Neighbor?"

"For your information, that only happened once, and her mom was having a Mary Kay party."

"Whatever," she says, lowering her voice.

Pottery may well be a fairly laid-back class, rulewise, but Ms. Mazur still insists on our speaking in hushed tones, for the sake of artistic concentration.

"Quick, one to ten, John Kenneally," she whispers.

"I refuse to play this game with you."

"Come on," she prods. "It's a brand-new year, we're juniors now, and word is he's available. Personally, I'd give him at least an eight-point-five for style, a seven for looks, and a nine for personality. The boy's a freakin' riot."

"Sorry to break this to you, but I'm not interested in John Kenneally."

"Then who, Snow White?"

I shake my head, still thinking about the boy from the parking lot—that sugary smell, those dark gray eyes.

And the way he touched me.

After the accident, after Gloria Beckham's full recovery—turns out she went into diabetic shock (hence her confusing the accelerator for the brake and whipping through the parking lot at a speed high enough to score her jail time in some states)—I scoured the school yearbooks, searching for the boy's identity.

Without any luck.

I pause a moment in my clay-wedging and reach down to touch the area below my navel, somehow still able to feel his fingers there.

"Okay, that's it!" Kimmie declares. "You really need to get yourself a man."

"Oh, please," I say, pretending just to be straightening

9

out the front of my apron. I run my fingers over a seam. "I wasn't doing anything scandalous."

"That's probably more hand action than you've gotten all year, isn't it? Forget it; I don't want to know. Here," she says, thrusting her verging-on-obscene clay man in front of me. "Say hello to Seymour. He's not perfect, but it's the best I can do on such short notice."

4

AT LUNCH, KIMMIE AND I CLAIM A much coveted spot on the upperclassmen side of the cafeteria—only two tables from the soda machines and just a sandwich crust's throw from the exit doors. A total score for midlisters like us—and one we intend to keep for the entire year.

Sitting with us is our friend Wes. We kind of adopted him during our freshman year, when the poor boy showed up at a Halloween dance dressed as a six-foot-long wiener. A couple of the lacrosse players thought it'd be funny to swipe his bun, making him look borderline offensive. Wes squawked to the chaperones. The lacrosse players got detentions. And that was how our good friend Wes earned the nickname of Wesley, the Oscar Mayer Whiner.

"Nice hair," Wes smirks, eyeing Kimmie's new pixie cut. She recently dyed it jet black and had more than sixteen inches hacked off for Locks of Love.

"For your information, it goes with my style."

"Oh, yeah, and what's that? Goth girl gone wrong?"

"Vintage vamp," she explains, gesturing to her outfit: a polka-dot dress circa 1960, combat boots, and a frilly red scarf. Thick black rings of Maybelline outline her pale blue eyes. "Laugh now, but it won't be so funny when I'm a rich and famous fashion designer with my own makeover show."

"Wait, will that makeover be for you?" Wes asks, pushing his glasses up on the bridge of his nose.

"Back off," I say, threatening him with a forkful of mac 'n' cheese, aimed and ready to launch at his mousse-infested brown hair.

"You'll never do it," he dares. "Just think about the mess that could leave on the table."

"The big, fat, *hairy* mess," Kimmie says, stifling a laugh.

"Especially when I retaliate with my meat loaf surprise." He smiles.

I drop my fork to my plate, avoiding a possible food fight.

"I take it we're feeling a little hostile today, Camelia Chameleon?" he asks.

"Very funny," I say, hating the sound of my name—and his incessant need to attach a reptile to it.

"And speaking of hostile," he continues, "did either of you hear about the new kid? Word is he's a killer."

"Killer hottie, I hope," Kimmie says, slipping a spoonful of peanut butter into her mouth.

"Killer as in *one who kills*," he explains. "Rumor has it, he nixed his girlfriend . . . pushed her off a cliff. The girl ended up landing against a rock and splattering to her bloody death."

"Sounds like someone's been watching too much *CSI*," Kimmie says.

"It's never too much," he snaps in his own defense.

"Wait," I say, pushing my mac 'n' cheese nastiness to the side. "What makes you think this rumor is true?"

"Oh, that's right." Kimmie grins. "Camelia doesn't believe in rumors . . . ever since they made that one up about her."

Wes laughs, knowing just what she's talking about. Freshman year, Jessica Peet, all pissy because I wouldn't let her cheat off my history test, decided to get me back by saying I made a habit out of peeing in the locker room shower rather than making the trip to the bathroom. For one whole quarter, I had people avoiding whatever shower stall I used.

Before I can defend myself, Matt comes and drops his books at the end of our table. "Hey, ladies," he says. "And Whiner." He nods at Wes.

"Who's laughing now?" I shoot Wes an evil smirk.

Matt and I used to date, but now we're just friends. People (like Kimmie) insist that he and I should give it another whirl, but honestly, we probably never should have *whirled* in the first place. It totally punctured a hole in our otherwise perfectly platonic friendship. And ever since, things haven't quite been the same between us.

"Aren't *we* looking spiffy this year?" Kimmie takes an oh-so-seductive bite of her peanut butter, slowly stripping Matt of the layers of Abercrombie he's sporting today.

Not so surprisingly, Matt doesn't take her visual molestation as a compliment. Instead, he ignores her and zeroes in on me. "Are we still on for study group this year? I could use some help in French."

"I guess," I say. "Let me check my schedule and see when I'm free."

Matt nods and leaves, and Kimmie gives me a kick under the table. "Have you gone mad?" she asks. "That boy's been working out. He's a total nine on a one-to-ten scale."

"If you like tall, blond, and chiseled, maybe," Wes says, nonchalantly pinching his itty-bitty bicep. "Personally, I think some girls prefer charm and personality."

"Too bad you fall short there, too, huh?" Kimmie says, giving Wes a wink.

"Matt and I are just friends," I remind her.

"Friends, schmends," she says. "What you need is a man."

I look up at the clock, suddenly eager for the bell to ring. And that's when I see him.

The boy from the parking lot.

I feel myself stand. I feel my heart jump up into my throat.

He sees me, too. I know he does.

"Um, Camelia, are you okay?" Kimmie asks, following my gaze.

"Check it out," Wes pipes up. "That's *him*—the guy who nixed his girlfriend."

The boy pauses, looking at me for just a second before turning away and walking out the door.

5

*H*IS NAME IS BEN CARTER.

I know because everybody at school is all abuzz about him. By fifth block of the day, not even three full hours after I first spotted him in the cafeteria, the story has grown into something you might see on a made-for-TV movie. People are saying Ben strangled his girlfriend before he pushed her over the cliff that day; that when the police searched his backpack they discovered a roll of duct tape, a ten-inch knife, and a list of other girls he'd wanted to attack.

It's last block of the day, a free block for Kimmie and me, and having snuck out of the library a few minutes early, we're standing just two classrooms away from Ben's locker, waiting for the bell to ring.

And waiting to see him again.

It's not that I'm some masochistic loony in love with the idea of hooking up with a former felon. It's just that I need to thank him—to look him in the eye, tell him that I appreciate the fact that he saved my life, and then walk away.

Instant closure.

"This is so very bold of you," Kimmie says, using her pencil as a hair pick. "I mean, let's face it, it might not even be the same guy."

"It is," I say, watching the second hand on the giant hallway clock. Only two minutes to go.

"So, you're convinced that a boy who supposedly murdered his girlfriend is the same one who saved your life?"

"You can't honestly tell me you believe all those rumors, can you? Besides, we don't know all the facts."

"Facts, schmacts." She rolls her eyes. "So he saved your life and touched your tummy. Lots of people have touched my random body parts, and you don't see *me* making such a big deal out of it."

"Last I checked saving someone's life *was* a big deal. Plus, it wasn't just that he touched me; it was the *way* he touched me."

"Oh, right." Kimmie yawns. "It gave you goose bumps and made your heart go pitter-pat. How could I forget?"

Instead of trying to make her understand what she clearly doesn't, I look back at the clock, watching the second hand get closer to twelve, wondering if I'll have the nerve to actually talk to him.

I close my eyes, anticipating the bell, and two seconds later it goes off—so loud I feel the vibration inside my gut.

The hallway fills with kids, people pushing by us,

probably annoyed that we're just standing there, holding up traffic.

But then I see him.

He hangs back for a bit, just loitering there, in the doorway of Senora Lynch's Spanish room, watching the herd go by.

"What's he doing?" Kimmie asks.

I shake my head and continue to watch, hoping to make eye contact, but he doesn't even look in my direction. Not once.

It's several minutes before the traffic in the hallway thins out even a little. And that's when he finally makes his way to his locker.

It's so obvious people notice him. As soon as they spot him, they gawk and exchange looks of sheer buzzery, like this is the biggest thing ever to rock our small-town world.

"Here's your chance." Kimmie nudges me. "It's either now or never."

"It's now," I say, my voice shaky.

I make my way toward him and my face flashes hot. Ben rips a piece of paper from his locker door, tosses it to the ground, and then works his padlock combination, totally ignoring the fact that I'm now standing right beside him.

"Ben?" I ask, feeling my pulse race. "Can I talk to you for a second?"

Still, he ignores me.

"Ben?" I repeat, a little louder this time.

Finally he peeks out from behind his locker door. "Can I help you?"

"Do you remember me?"

He shakes his head and looks away—back into his locker to search for something.

"Three months ago," I continue, trying to jog his memory. "In the parking lot, behind the school . . . a car was coming toward me, and you pushed me out of the way."

"Sorry," he mumbles.

"You saved my life," I whisper, catching a glimpse of the paper he tossed to the floor—a torn notebook scrap with the word *murderer* scribbled across it. "The car would've hit me otherwise."

"I honestly have no idea what you're talking about." He slams his locker door shut.

"It was *you*," I blurt out, as if he couldn't possibly have forgotten something so significant.

"Not me," he insists. "You obviously have me confused with somebody else."

I shake my head and focus on his face—on his almond-shaped eyes and the sharpness of his jaw. He runs his fingers through his hair—out of frustration, maybe—and that's when I see it.

The scar on his forearm.

My eyes widen, and my heart beats with new intensity.

Ben sees that I've spotted the scar and lowers his arm, buries his hand in his pocket. "I gotta go," he says, glancing over his shoulder.

Throngs of people have collected around us: Davis Miller and his boy-band cohorts, a group of girls on the softball team, a couple of boys on their way to detention, and a bunch of drama rats en route to the theater.

"I just wanted to say thank you," I say, deciding to forget them.

"It wasn't me," he says and then turns away.

Leaving me once again.

6

I want to talk to her. I had the perfect opportunity, but I messed things up. She's just so perfect—so sweet, so shy, so amazingly hot—that I get all nervous.

It's easier to watch her in private, like at the library. I hid behind the stacks, imagining what it'd be like to take her someplace nice. I pictured her sitting in a fancy restaurant, waiting for me to arrive, instead of sitting in the library, cooped up in school.

I noticed she'd chosen the table that looks out onto the courtyard. She kept gazing out at it, like she wanted to be outside.

What I'd give to be with her—to walk with her over fallen leaves, to hear the crunch beneath our feet, and then to kiss her, the cool autumn breeze whipping around us.

In time I know it'll happen. I'll make it happen. Or else I'll die trying.

"OKAY, SO WHAT DID HE SAY?" Kimmie asks. "I want *every* word."

We're sitting in one of the booths at Brain Freeze, the ice-cream shop down the street from our school.

"Oh, my God, *wait*," she says, just as soon as I open my mouth to speak. "Did you see John Kenneally?"

I peer around at the other booths.

"Not *here*," she squawks, dragging the word out for three full syllables. "In the hallway, while you were talking to that Ben guy. He was totally scoping the scene. It looked like he wanted to talk to you. He was so close to tapping you on the shoulder, but you turned the other way."

"I didn't notice."

Kimmie sighs. "Leave it to you to miss a hottie like him. If *you* don't go for him, I totally will."

"He's all yours," I say, taking a bite of my mocha-licious mud.

"So what did he say?" she asks.

"John?"

"*No*—that Ben guy."

"Not much. Just that it wasn't him—that I have him confused with someone else."

"See, I told you," she sings.

"But he's lying," I continue. "I *know* it was him."

"Why would he lie about something like that?" Kimmie takes a sip of her peanut butter frappe.

I shrug. "Maybe he's one of those superprivate people; maybe that's why he took off after he saved me in the first place."

"Doubtful," she says. "I mean, think about it: if you were accused of murder, wouldn't you welcome an opportunity where people could see you saving someone?"

"Sounds pretty serious," Wes says, sneaking up from behind me. Spoon and straw in hand, he pulls up a chair and takes the liberty of mooching off our desserts. "Word's out that you were harassing Killer Boy after school today."

"Where did you hear that?" I ask, knocking his spoon away.

"People." He smirks.

"What people?"

Wes's smirk grows into a full-blown smile, exposing the tiny chip in his front tooth. "Everybody's talkin' about it."

"You're such a lame-o," Kimmie says. "We've only been out of school for an hour."

"Doesn't matter." He readjusts his wire-rimmed glasses. "I have ears . . . and eyes."

"Stalking the girls' softball team again?" Kimmie tsk-tsks. "You know how tacky that is, don't you?"

Wes shrugs, obviously caught.

"My vote is that you forget about Touch Boy," Kimmie says, pointing at me with her straw.

"Unless of course you want to wind up being the next victim of the week," Wes adds. "Better start wearing clean underwear. You never know when you might end up lying half naked somewhere."

"Good advice." Kimmie nods.

"I'm nobody's victim," I say.

"You can victimize me." He gives his spoon a good lick.

"Whatever," I say, choosing to ignore him. "Forgetting Ben is a whole lot easier said than done. I saw the scar."

"Wait, what scar?" Kimmie asks.

I tell them about the scar I saw on Ben's forearm earlier—how I recognized it from the day he saved me.

"Do I smell a scandal coming on?" Wes asks, making his voice all gruff and deep.

Kimmie sniffs in Wes's direction. "That stench isn't scandalous . . . it's downright venomous."

Wes takes an extra-large sip of her frappe in retaliation.

"Forget him, Camelia," Kimmie says. "I mean, yes, he

24

saved your life; it was very chivalrous of him. And, yes, he's totally buff, which further complicates things, but closure is way overrated, in my opinion, anyway."

"Maybe you're right." I sigh, sinking back into my seat.

"No 'maybe' about it. Preoccupy yourself with someone yummier," she insists.

"Like who? Matt or John Kenneally?"

"Well, since you bring them up . . ."

I roll my eyes in response.

"Oh, but that's right," she continues. "Matt was no good, as I recall. He called you all the time, gave you sweet little gifts—"

"Made you homemade chicken soup when you were sick," Wes adds.

"It wasn't edible," I say, remembering the mystery gray chunks.

"Whatever," Kimmie argues. "Give me a boy who can open up a can of Chef Boyardee, and I'm his."

"I've got a Twistaroni with your name all over it," Wes jokes.

"Matt was nice," I say to be clear. "But there comes a point when nice is *too* nice—too clingy, even before we started dating."

"Right," he says. "What you need is a malicious killer."

On that note, I excuse myself from the table and leave, since I promised my mother I'd help her with dinner tonight anyway.

Ever since I took a part-time job at Knead, the pottery shop downtown, my mom's been all fanatical about the two of us having enough mother-daughter bonding time. And so it's become our ritual—at least once a week, on a day I'm not working, we join forces to prepare dinner.

"We're making summer squash pasta with soy butter and basil sauce, date-nut logs, and fresh kale-rot juice," my mother announces, just as soon as I come through the door.

"Kale-rot?"

She nods and pulls one of my pottery bowls down from the cabinet—the widemouthed blue one with the yellow pinwheel swirls. "It's made with carrots and kale."

"Sounds delectable," I lie.

My mom's sort of a health freak, from her henna red hair to her organic cotton sneakers. As a result, my dad and I end up at the drive-through of Taco Bell at least twice a week.

"Come on," she says, waving me to the island. "I want to hear all about your first day of school. Any cute boys? Inspiring teachers? How was your lunch?"

"Negative; not a one; and nauseating," I say, picking at my pearl-colored nail polish.

"Now, there's a healthy attitude."

"I'm exaggerating." I slide onto a stool. "Well, sort of."

My mother, still in her yoga gear from work, takes a deep and cleansing breath, followed by a sip of her homemade dandelion tea. "Do you want to talk about it?"

"Maybe another time," I say, thinking about Ben.

"Well, then, do you want to come to my full-moon meeting tonight? You might find it cleansing." She sweeps a cluster of corkscrew curls from in front of her dark green eyes.

"No thanks," I say, since a night of barking at the moon and impromptu belly dancing is hardly what *I'd* call cleansing.

Mom nods and looks away, down at her container of dates. She dumps the entire package into the food processor and then goes to click on the power.

"Aren't you forgetting something?" I ask.

It takes her a moment, but then she notices. She forgot to pit the dates first—a culinary offense I committed way back when we were trying to make raw fudge.

Mom scoops the dates out, her eyes all teary, like the possibility of having a dull food-processing blade is the worst thing in the world.

"Mom?"

"Aunt Alexia called today," she says, in an effort to explain her tears.

"Oh," I say, steeling myself for the blow.

She wipes her eyes, trying to regain composure. "It wasn't anything bad. She just sounded kind of off, that's all."

"Aunt Alexia *is* kind of off."

"She's working now," she continues, "trying to stay busy, to get her life back on track. She goes to a therapy group twice a week and painting classes every Saturday afternoon."

"Then what?"

Mom shakes her head. The corners of her mouth quiver downward. And for just a second she looks like she's going to lose it all over again. "She's fine," she says, finally. "I'm sure of it."

She follows up with a deep yoga breath and then starts pitting the dates.

"Mom?" I ask, sensing her angst.

But she clearly doesn't want to talk about it, instead ordering me to peel the squash, soak the basil, grind the nuts. It isn't long before we've whipped up a dish worthy of Sir Paul-vegan-McCartney himself. I take a stack of plates and start to set the table. And that's when I notice a large manila envelope addressed to me, sitting atop my mother's Buddha beads. I pick it up, noticing right away that it wasn't even mailed. It has no postage, no postmark, and nil for a return address. Still, I rip it open and pull out the contents.

It's a photo of me, standing outside of school this morning; I can tell by my outfit. Someone's printed it on a glossy eight-by-ten sheet of paper and drawn a bubbly red heart around my body.

I flip the picture over in search of a name or message, but it's blank. "Did somebody drop this off for me today?"

My mother shakes her head. "It was in the mailbox, with everything else."

"And when did you pick up the mail?" I ask, wondering

when someone would have had the time—between the end of school and now—to develop a picture and drop it off at my house.

She pauses from kale-rot-juicing to look up at me. "Around five, just before you got home. Why, what is it?"

I flash the photo at her. "Probably just a joke."

"Looks more like a secret admirer."

I run my fingers over it, thinking about this morning in front of the school, and trying to remember who I saw hanging around.

"Camelia, are you okay?" My mother pushes. "Did something happen at school?"

I shrug, tempted to tell her about Ben—about all the alleged rumors I heard about him—but it seems she's too preoccupied now, her eyes fixed on a big, empty bowl.

"Just the usual first-day-back stuff." I return the photo to its envelope and head to my room to give Kimmie a call.

There may be no return address, but a stunt like this definitely has her name written all over it.

8

"I HAVE NO IDEA WHAT YOU'RE EVEN talking about," Kimmie tells me.

Unable to reach her the night before, I end up hunting her down before homeroom. We're standing in an alcove of lockers, and I'm providing cover while she stuffs the front of her dress with enough tissue paper to wrap Christmas presents in for the next two years.

"I didn't leave anything in your mailbox," she continues, "least of all a picture of you with a heart around it. I mean, come on, how cheesy-nineteen-seventies-stalker-movie is that?"

"Are you sure? I won't be mad."

"Seriously, Camelia." She rolls her eyes and checks her bust in her locker mirror. "If I were weirdo enough to go running around taking pictures of people behind their backs, do you honestly think I'd start with you? No offense, of course."

"None taken."

"I mean, let's face it," she continues. "I can take pictures of *you* anytime. The boys' swim team, on the other hand . . . now that's a different story." She slams her locker door shut, her palms positioned over her stuffed chest, trying to get herself somewhat proportionate.

"Need another tissue?" I ask, noticing how Righty appears just a wee bit plumper than its partner.

Kimmie plucks out a tissue for good measure. "There, now, how do I look? The dress is new—for me, anyway. The saleslady told me it's vintage 1950. I'm thinking about designing a jumpsuit version of it."

It's a jet black, cap-sleeved, knee-length number, with a giant silver bow that sits at the waist.

"Very cute."

"It's beyond cute," she says, correcting me. "It makes me feel like a walking present."

I'm tempted to ask her if that explains all the tissue paper, but I bite my tongue instead.

"Now, who shall be my birthday boy?" She scopes the hallway for prospective victims, her eyes zeroing in on John Kenneally standing across the hall in a throng of his soccer teammates. John bends down to tie his shoelace, sending Kimmie into an absolute tizzy.

"So beautiful." She places her hand over her well-insulated chest, completely taken aback. "I mean, honestly, how does one get an ass like that? So firm . . . so symmetrical."

"Unlike your gift-wrapped boobs."

"Excuse me?"

"I hate to break this to you, but I have way more pressing issues to contend with than John Kenneally's butt cheeks."

"Oh, yeah? Like what?"

"Maybe Wes left it," I press on, refusing to drop the whole photo issue.

"Left what?" she mutters, still eyeing John.

"Forget it," I sigh.

"Wait, are we still talking about the picture?"

In her mind, John must be down to his Skivvies by now. "Yeah, it was probably Wes," she continues. "He *is* taking photography this year. Plus, he's done stupid stuff like this before. Last year he left a Saran Wrapped rubber Teletubby in my duffel bag, along with a note that said, 'Save me. I'm suffocating.'"

"I'm not even going to ask."

"Bottom line—I wouldn't obsess over it, especially when there are way more delectable things to obsess over." She stares longingly at John.

"You're hopeless," I tell her.

"Hopelessly in love." She fans herself with her anatomy lab book, which is oddly apropos, considering that the front cover has a picture of the human heart on it.

"The weird thing," I continue, "is that the picture was taken yesterday. I recognized my outfit, meaning whoever took it developed it the same day it was left in my mailbox."

"So?" she says. "Ever hear of one-hour photo?"

"Actually, I think someone printed it at home. It looked a little rough around the edges."

"That's the beauty of digital photography—no middleman, no wait time, and no worries about getting even your most incriminating photos developed. Remember the time I took that picture of my butt in the mirror? The store where I went to have it developed deleted the negative completely."

"Tragic."

"You bet it was. So much for my Christmas card idea."

"I have to go," I say, checking the hallway clock. There's only a minute left before homeroom, and I have a full two-minute walk to get there.

I turn to leave, but not even three steps away, I end up smacking right into John Kenneally's chest. "Sorry," I say, wondering how that just happened, and noticing how his clothes smell like peony-scented musk.

"No worries." He smiles. "I enjoyed it." He lingers for just a moment too long before finally continuing down the hallway.

A second later, Kimmie twirls me back around to face her. "Oh my god, I absolutely *hate* you," she says. "What did it feel like? What did he smell like?"

"Kimmie," I say, "get a grip."

"A grip around him, I hope."

I watch John walk down the hallway. At the same moment, he turns to look back. He waves in our direction, and I wave back. But Kimmie, too busy fanning herself again, doesn't even notice.

IN CHEMISTRY, I LOITER TOWARD the back of the room, waiting for everybody to file in. Mr. Swenson (nicknamed Mr. Sweat-man, for obvious reasons), has this rule that, whoever you choose to sit with on the first day of class becomes your lab partner for the entire year.

Needless to say, seat selection is definitely critical.

Since the sciences, collectively it seems, aren't really my strong suit, I search around for someone who I think might do well with things like beakers, test tubes, and Bunsen burners.

Until I finally see her—Rena Maruso, the girl who helped get me through bio.

"Hey," I say, waving her over. I gesture to a table in the back and sit down. "We can be lab partners again this year."

But Rena appears less than delighted to see me, despite

my stellar organization skills. She may not want to admit it, but thanks to me, we always handed in the neatest, most orderly lab reports.

"It won't be so bad," I say, trying to assure her. "At least this year we won't have to dissect anything, right?"

I know she must still blame me for accidentally spilling my Gatorade on that poor dead frog. Not only did it score us a big fat goose egg on our lab report, but I also got detention for having an open drink container in class.

Rena scans the room to see who's left, but it seems people have quickly paired off. She lets out a sigh and finally sits down, stacking her books between us to mark her personal science-loving territory. But after a few moments, when everybody has pretty much settled into their places, she switches seats, spotting an open chair at the front of the room, right beside tree-hugging, save-the-planet Tate Williams.

Just perfect.

I look up at the Sweat-man, waiting for him to announce the inevitable: that I'll have the unequivocal pleasure (not) of pairing up with him this year for my labs— of having to smell his sweaty self and be subjected to the fly-away dandruff in his hair. (*Note to self*: wear lab smock.)

But then Ben walks in.

He hands a slip of paper to the Sweat-man, probably denoting his enrollment in our class. A couple of snickers come from the corner of the room. Mr. Swenson checks and rechecks the slip of paper, comparing it to his attendance list, as if maybe there's some mistake.

"Take a seat," Sweat-man finally says. He scratches his head, releasing at least a tablespoon of dandruff over his shoulders.

Ben searches the room, and so do I, but the only remaining chair is the one beside mine.

He sees it and our eyes lock.

"Is there a problem, Mr. Carter?" The Sweat-man is glaring at him.

Ben just stands there at the front of the room. Staring at me. Making my face go hot and my palms clammy.

"No problem," he says, finally.

He joins me at my table, but he doesn't look at me again for the entire block.

Not once.

Even though I want him to.

Even though I know I shouldn't.

THE FOLLOWING DAY IN CHEMISTRY, Sweat-man starts prepping us for our first lab, saying that we need to work as two-person teams, that any slackdom affects not only ourselves but also our partners, blah-blah-blah.

I really want to talk to Ben.

He looks more amazing than usual today in a pair of artfully tattered jeans and a faded blue T-shirt. His skin is a bit darker, too, like maybe he's been spending time out in the sun.

He sits down beside me and starts paging through his notes.

"Hi," I venture.

He nods, but he doesn't look at me; just keeps flipping pages back and forth.

And so I look even closer and admire him even more— his tousled dark hair and the scruff on his chin; his strong, broad shoulders and the muscles in his forearm. I try to think up something clever to say, but all I can come up with is: "Do you have any Wite-Out?"

Without so much as glancing in my direction, Ben reaches into his bag and slides the little white bottle across the table at me.

"Thanks," I say, noticing the dimple in his chin, and how he smells like melon soap. Not knowing what to do with the Wite-Out, I resort to blotting my name from the inside cover of my notebook. "Did you do the homework last night?" I ask, passing the bottle back to him.

He nods.

"Well that's good, because Mr. Swenson lives for pop quizzes. You never know when he might spring one on us—hence the word 'pop.'"

Ben doesn't say anything. He just keeps reading over his notes, probably thinking I'm a complete and utter idiot because, let's face it, I certainly sound like one.

After class, he starts to pack things up but ends up leaving the Wite-Out on the table.

"Hey," I say, tapping him on the shoulder before he can sneak away.

Ben whirls around and takes a step back. "Don't," he snaps.

I gesture to the Wite-Out. "You forgot something," I say, feeling stupid for even trying to be nice.

Ben rebounds with an apology. His eyes soften, and his lips form a smile, but it's far too little and way too late, and so I ignore him and hurry out the door.

* * *

Later, for free period, I decide to go to the library, determined to get to the bottom of Ben's story. Armed and ready with notepad and pen, I claim a computer in the corner and start googling his name, along with the words *murder*, *accident*, and *cliff*.

A bunch of Ben Carters pop up: Ben Carter, astrophysicist; Ben Carter, real estate mogul; Ben Carter, whose Web page shows a picture of a forty-five-year-old guy looking for love.

I let out a sigh, wondering if my lack of luck is because Ben was a minor at the time of the incident—if maybe the press was trying to protect his privacy. I'm just about to call it a day when I feel something touch my back.

I jump in my seat and swivel around—only to find Matt.

"Hey, there," he says, taking a step back as if I've scared him, too. "I didn't mean to startle you."

"It's okay," I say, mentally peeling myself off the ceiling.

He stands there a few moments, shuffling his feet like the mere sight of me makes him nervous.

But I guess I'm nervous, too. I wish things could go back to the way they were at the pre-dating stage—when he was Matthieu and I was Camille and we were each other's role-playing buddies in French class.

"What's up?" I ask him.

"I'm sorry I didn't call you last night."

I feel my brow furrow in confusion as I suddenly flash

back to the end of last year—when he used to call me at least twice a day.

"About French tutoring," he continues.

"Oh, right."

"I mean, I hate to bother you. It's just that you know how I suck at French, and I have Madame Funkenwilder this year. I hear she's a real hard-ass."

"She is." I giggle, suddenly wishing my science skills were even half as good as my linguistic ones.

"So, do you think you could help out? I mean, I could pay you. I just don't want to screw up my GPA, and I have a quiz next Tuesday." He glances over my shoulder at the computer screen.

"Don't worry about it," I say, doing my best to rebound. I grab the computer mouse to shut things down, but the evidence is right there in the search-engine box.

Matt pulls up a chair and sits. "You heard about that guy, huh?" he says, obviously having spotted Ben's name.

"Who hasn't?"

"So, why are you checking him out?"

"He's my lab partner this year," I say, forgoing the whole saving-my-life story.

"And you're nervous about him?"

"I'm *curious* about him," I clarify.

Matt smiles slightly. His teal blue eyes look right into mine, making me smile, too.

"What?" I ask, feeling my cheeks start to blaze.

"I know you, Camelia, remember?"

"*And?*"

"And let me help you. I'll find out this guy's deal."

"There is no deal. I was just curious," I remind him.

"So, let me *un*-curious you." He smiles wider, smoothing back a strand of his dirty-blond hair. "I have connections, you know." He winks at me, all covertlike. "It's the least I can do as thanks for helping me out with French."

"Well, don't lose any sleep over it or anything."

He nods. His eyes linger a moment on my flushed cheeks. We make plans to study together Monday night. "I'll swing by after my movie date with Rena," he says. "Did you know the theater downtown shows Hitchcock flicks every Monday afternoon?"

I shake my head. "I didn't even know you were dating Rena Maruso." Pretty, pert, petite, good-at-science Rena Maruso.

"Well, yeah," he says, like it's so incredibly yesterday's news.

And, no, it's not that I'm jealous. I just don't want to hear about Rena Maruso, or anyone else who might be dating my ex, for that matter—especially when said ex is being *so* nice, almost making me forget why we broke up in the first place.

Almost.

II

*I*T'S THE LAST BLOCK OF THE DAY, and everyone's talking about Ben's locker. Sometime before lunch there was another sign left on it. Only this time, Ben couldn't just tear it down. Someone had written the words *Killer Go Home* down the length of the door in permanent black marker.

The sign was up there for two full hours before Mr. Snell, the school principal, ordered a janitor to come and cover it up with a few strokes of red paint.

"Remember last year," Kimmie says, applying a fresh coat of my peach-colored lip gloss, "when Polly Piranha got vandalized?"

Since our English teacher is out sick today, Kimmie, Wes, and I have the rare treat of an extra free block. And so we're sitting in the courtyard behind the school—basically a glorified asphalt driveway with a bunch of picnic tables set up—pretending to do our homework.

I laugh, still able to picture it—the giant wooden cutout of a piranha, our school mascot, with boobs spray-painted right over her fins. Poor Polly had apparently sat in the same spot by the football field for more than thirty years, and this was the first time she'd sported hooters.

"Yeah," I say, "but in that case Snell had her taken down within minutes."

"A damned shame." Wes shakes his head. "Those were some nice hooters."

"The only ones you'll ever see up close," Kimmie says.

"Um, excuse me, but haven't you ever heard of *Playboy*?" he asks.

"Haven't *you* ever heard of *hard-up* boy?"

"I wonder how the truth even leaked out about Ben," I say, cutting through their banter.

"Are you kidding?" Wes squawks. "This is a small town, with even smaller minds. A guy can't even scratch the wrong way without people suspecting he's got a killer case of the crabs."

"Something you want to tell us about?" Kimmie asks.

Wes gives her the middle-finger nose scratch.

"Well, if this town is so small," I ask, "how come nobody told me Matt was dating Rena Maruso?"

"What?" Kimmie's jaw drops.

"Apparently true. I talked to him earlier."

"Not true," Kimmie protests. "Rena's in my Spanish class. The girl tells me everything."

"Maybe she only tells you *some* things," Wes says.

"Or maybe Matt's trying to make you jealous,"

Kimmie says. "It's the oldest trick in the book."

"Well, whatever," I say, eager to get back to business. "I've been asking people about him."

"Matt?" Kimmie perks up.

"No, Ben."

"Okay, so, no offense," she says, "but does this fascination with Ben have anything to do with you deciding to give up your senior-citizen way of life?"

"Senior citizen?"

"Yeah, you know, safe, habitual, carefully planned, doesn't like surprises, likes to be in before dark—"

"You have to admit, you are a bit of an old lady," Wes adds.

"Of course, we love that about you," Kimmie insists.

"Right," Wes says. "I mean, who doesn't love their grandma? And it could explain your sudden fixation with Danger Boy."

"Hold up," Kimmie says. "If Ben were a *real* danger boy, who *really* killed his girlfriend, do you honestly think they'd allow him back in school?"

"You don't think he did it?" I ask.

"What I think is that you're starting to sound just a tad bit obsessed."

"Well, it's a little hard not to be. I mean, Ben's name is everywhere—in practically every conversation."

"In practically every girl's worst nightmare," Wes says, creepifying his voice by making it superdeep. He uses a pencil as a makeshift knife to jab at the air.

"Well, dangerous or not," Kimmie says, popping a

fireball candy into her mouth, "the boy is hot—for an alleged killer, that is."

"Why is it that all the good ones have to be killers?" Wes lets out an exaggerated sigh.

"You're such a spaz," I say, throwing a corn chip at his head. It sticks in his mousse-laden hair, but he picks it out and eats it anyway.

"So, what did you find out about him, Nancy Drew?" Kimmie asks me.

"Nothing reliable." I shrug. "The stories are getting more ridiculous by the minute."

Wes nods. "Last I heard, the boy chopped up his entire family and ate them for breakfast."

"That's sick," Kimmie says.

"But tasty." He thieves a handful of my corn chips.

"Speaking of sick," I say, "what was up with the photo you left in my mailbox?"

"Photo?"

I nod. "The one of me . . . in front of the school . . . with a heart around it."

He tilts his head, visibly confused. "*Qué*?"

"Don't be a dick," Kimmie says. "Fess up. It was you. Just like it was you with that Teletubby stunt."

"Honestly," he says, "dicks and Teletubbies aside, I have absolutely no idea what you're even talking about."

"Hold up," I say. "You didn't leave a photo of me in my mailbox?"

Wes shakes his head.

"Aren't you taking photography this year?" I ask.

"And so, what does that prove—that I'm suddenly taking random pictures of people and leaving them in their mailboxes?"

"I wouldn't worry about it." Kimmie spits her fireball into her palm. "It's probably just some lame-o's idea of a joke." She shoots Wes an evil look.

"Hey, don't look at this lame-o," he says, pointing out the front of his T-shirt, where the words *Innocent Until Proven Guilty* are printed across the chest.

12

I've been seeing her a lot lately, making it a point to be wherever she is.

I wonder if she can feel my eyes watching her—crawling over her skin, memorizing the zigzag part of her hair and the way her hips sway from side to side when she walks.

There's so much I want to ask her about, like if she sleeps on the left side of the bed or the right, and what color her toothbrush is.

And if she liked the picture I left in her mailbox. I wish I'd been there when she opened the envelope. I'd love to have seen her expression—if she bit her bottom lip like she does when she gets nervous. If she hugged the photo against her chest, imagining someone like me. Or if her lips curled up into a smile worthy of a magazine cover.

I took that picture from across the street, standing at the side of the telephone building. I had my camera set to zoom as I waited for the perfect angle.

She looked so nervous. She kept fidgeting with her bag strap and twisting her fingers through her long blond hair.

But who am I to talk? I get nervous, too. Whenever I see her, I can barely think straight. I try to calm myself down—to remind myself to be patient, to not be too anxious, that I'll soon have everything I want.

Inside my head, I chant, "Calm, calm, calm."

13

IT'S FRIDAY AFTERNOON, and I'm sitting in chemistry class, doing my best to focus, to take Kimmie's advice about chalking the whole mysterious photo issue up to some lame-o's idea of a joke, since, after all, she's probably right.

It's the first lab session of the year, and Ben and I have a handful of test tubes set up in front of us, along with a graduated cylinder and a couple of teaspoons. The goal: to perform, discuss, and record the reactions that occur based on the mixture of a few choice chemicals.

I'm trying my hardest to concentrate, to tell myself that combining distilled water with sodium bicarbonate is the most important thing in the world right now, even though Ben is watching and recording my every move.

My hand shakes slightly as I add in a couple of teaspoons of phenolphthalein, which according to the Sweat-man, was formerly used in over-the-counter laxatives. I glance over at Missy and Chrissy Tompkin, otherwise known as the Laxative Twins, wondering if they're going to try and pocket a stash for later.

"Thirsty?" I ask Ben, holding the mixture up like a drink. The addition of the laxative stuff has made the solution resemble fruit punch.

But he doesn't think it's funny. "Add in two grams of calcium chloride," he says, keeping things all clinical-like.

"Don't forget," Sweat-man announces. "This lab isn't just about your visual senses here. What does the test-tube glass feel like with each added substance? Does it get heavier in comparison to the other tubes? Does it get cold or heat up? Is there any change in smell? Do you hear anything?"

I look up at Ben, realizing we've completely omitted the whole touchy-feely aspect of the experiment.

"Do you want to hold it?" I ask, extending the tube out to him.

Ben looks at it but shakes his head, continuing to read me the directions from his lab book.

"Wait," I say. "We need to record this stuff—our reactions, what we observe."

"Can't you just record it for the both of us?"

I try not to let his slacking bother me, especially since, as far as things look in everybody else's tubes, it appears as though we're doing everything right. I jot down my observations and then, following the instructions as Ben reads them aloud, I add in a couple more ingredients, finally topping the solution off with nitric acid and bromothymol blue.

The solution in the tube starts to fizzle and heat up, and the color changes from pink to yellow.

"You really should feel this," I say, holding the tube out to him again.

But Ben has his own idea of fizzle: "I'm all set," he says.

"Not exactly a team player, are you, Mr. Carter?" The Sweat-man is standing right behind him now.

Ben glances at the tube again, and for five full seconds I think he's going to take it, but instead he says: "I've already felt it."

"Oh, really?" Sweat-man scratches his head, and I step back to avoid the flurry of flakes. "So, how would you describe the temperature of the tube?" he asks.

Ben shrugs. "Kind of cold."

The Sweat-man makes his infamous game-show-buzzer sound, denoting the wrong answer. "You really should have phoned a friend."

"Why don't you feel it again?" I say, in an effort to play nice. I hand him the tube, just as the Sweat-man walks away. But Ben's still being all weird. His fingers linger in the air, just inches from mine. "Take it," I say, all but placing the tube into his hand.

He finally does. And his hand accidentally grazes mine. I feel the skin of his thumb rub against my middle finger.

The next thing I know, Ben drops the tube. It shatters on the floor. Yellow solution spills out everywhere.

Ben takes a step back, breathing hard.

"It's no big deal," I tell him.

But he doesn't respond. He just stands there, staring at me. His dark gray eyes are wide and insistent.

"Real slick," Sweat-man says. "Clean it up—*now*."

Ben doesn't move. So I grab a mop from the corner of the room and start to clean up the mess.

And that's when he touches me.

His hand glides down my forearm and encircles my wrist, hard, making my heart beat fast and my pulse start to race. I open my mouth to say something—to ask what he's doing, to tell him to let go—but nothing comes out.

"Shhh," Ben says. He takes a step closer, his eyes fixed on mine. I can feel the heat of his breath on my neck.

"Hey, check it out," I hear someone whisper.

Still, I don't look away. Because I honestly don't want to.

A smattering of giggles erupts in the classroom, catching the attention of Sweat-man at the front of the room. He makes a beeline for our table and butts his sweaty self between us as Ben releases his grip on my forearm.

"Did he hurt you?" Sweat-man asks.

I shake my head, feeling a slight sting in my wrist from Ben's grip. After a few awkward moments, Sweat-man orders me to finish cleaning up, and then he orders Ben to the office.

"No," I balk. "It's fine. I'm fine. He was only trying to help me." I look down at the mess on the floor.

But Ben doesn't question the order. He just collects his books, takes one last look at me, and then scurries out of the room.

$\mathcal{E}$VEN THOUGH I'M NOT scheduled to work at Knead today, I end up going there right after school.

I just have to get away.

Spencer, my boss, can sense my moodiness as soon as the doorbells announce my arrival.

"Here," he says, handing me a mound of clay. "Sculpt your way to a happier self."

Spencer is the greatest—totally laid back and unbelievably talented. You'd never know it from his hard-as-nails exterior—complete with straggly long hair, torn up jeans, and a three-inch scar down the side of his face—but he sculpts the most feminine of figurines using the most unyielding of materials.

I take his clay-mound offering but refrain from telling him that it's not exactly unhappiness I'm dealing with right now. It's confusion. I mean, why did Ben touch me like that? Why was he being so weird in lab? And what's with all the mixed signals?

"Is it a guy?" Spencer asks, setting up the tables for tonight's pottery class.

I nod and slip on an apron.

"Care to elaborate? I can give you the male perspective— free of charge, of course."

"Maybe after I wedge," I say, slamming the clay down on my work board.

Spencer is barely twenty-five, but he's owned this shop for a little over two years now. I first met him during my freshman year, when he was substituting for Ms. Mazur, his supposed mentor—something he does only sparingly now that he has the shop. He told me I was a natural with the potter's wheel and asked if I wanted a job. About a year and a half later—the time it took me to convince my parents I was responsible enough to handle work *and* school— I finally took him up on it.

And it's been my dream job ever since.

After only three weeks of working for him, he gave me free run of the place: "So you can work on your stuff whenever inspiration hits," he said, dropping the shop's keys into my palm, "be it eleven o'clock at night or three in the morning." And, though I've yet to take him up on the generous offer to work whenever I please, I have a feeling those days are coming.

I honestly can't remember another time in my life when I felt this unhinged.

"Will you be needing something a bit stronger than

that?" Spencer asks, referring to the clay. "A little maple wood? Or some iron, maybe?"

"No," I smile, giving my clay another good thwack against the board. "This will do just fine."

Spencer gives me a thumbs-up and then leaves me alone. But I'm not alone for long. Not even ten minutes later, Kimmie comes bursting through the door. "I knew I'd find you here," she announces.

"Is something wrong?"

She sets her design portfolio down against the table with a thud. "I'll say something's wrong. You didn't even call me. Word is he practically took you down in chemistry."

"Wait—*what*?"

"Everybody's talking about it—about him—and how he tried to maul you today."

"Ben?"

"Was there someone else who tried to maul you?"

"That's not how it happened," I say, squeezing and resqueezing my clay in an effort to remain calm.

"I know, because apparently you didn't even put up a fight. *Apparently* you didn't even seem to mind."

"He touched me again," I say, my heart tightening at the mere words.

"From what I heard, it was way more than just a touch." She folds her arms and taps her patent-leather Mary Jane against the linoleum floor.

"No," I say. "You don't understand. He *touched* me, like in the parking lot that day—and it got all weird."

"Weird as in creepy?"

"Weird as in unbelievable," I say, still able to picture it, to picture him—the way our faces were only inches apart and how his bottom lip quivered when he told me to shush. "It's like he touches me on my arm or my stomach, but my whole body feels it."

"Honestly, Camelia, do you know how cheesy that sounds? Even for you."

"You know what I mean. I need to know what he's all about."

"Is everything okay?" Spencer asks, inserting himself into our conversation. I glance toward his work area at the back of the shop, wondering how long he's been standing behind us and how much he actually heard.

"Better than okay," Kimmie says, openly admiring his Rambo-like physique. "Especially if you'll be substituting for Ms. Mazur anytime soon. I'd love to show you my technique. I call it the thump-and-slap."

"Sounds like you're having fun. Maybe if Ms. Mazur calls in sick."

"I'll see what I can do," she says, practically drooling. "Camelia, do we know anyone with whooping cough? I hear it's supercatchy."

"I'll just pretend I didn't hear that," I say.

"I'm heading out to pick up some molds," Spencer says. "I shouldn't be more than an hour. Camelia, will you be around when I get back?" A lock of his wavy dark hair falls into his eyes, turning Kimmie to virtual mush. "I thought maybe we could talk about stuff."

"Talk is cheap," Kimmie interrupts. "Don't you have anything to show?"

"As in, what I'm working on?" Spencer asks.

"For starters."

"Well, I'm about to begin sculpting a six-foot-tall ballerina in bronze."

"Need a model?" She stands on her tiptoes. "I could wear my stilettos."

"I'll keep it in mind," he says, and turns to me. "So, will I see you later?"

"I don't know," I say, glancing at his hand. It still lingers on my shoulder. "I kind of have a lot of homework."

"On a Friday?" Kimmie asks.

"So, maybe another time," he says, reminding me to lock up when I'm done.

Kimmie bops me on the head with a sponge once he's gone. "Honestly, what is your problem?"

"You're the one with the problem. What are you doing hitting on my boss?"

"*He* was hitting on *you*," she says, correcting me.

"No way," I say. "Spencer's just like that . . . he's just *nice*."

"Yeah, well, nice boss plus open invitation to hang out after hours equals a very happy lizard . . . meaning you, Miss Chameleon. You want a spicier life? Well, then, he's your chipotle pepper."

"I am *so* not interested in Spencer."

"Because he didn't supposedly kill anybody?"

"Okay, I'm done having this conversation." I roll my clay up into a ball and plop it down against my wedging board.

"Fine," she says, drying her hands. She tosses the wad of paper towels to the floor, in lieu of the garbage barrel, and it catches on her heel. "Call me later."

"Will do," I say, watching as she walks off, the roll of paper towels trailing along after her like industrial-strength toilet paper, totally making me giggle.

15

She's become my addiction and she doesn't even know it. Part of me wants her to know—wants her to feel me out there. Watching her. Checking how she dresses. And what she eats. And who she spends her time with. Watching as she opens her bedroom curtains first thing in the morning. And walks to school. And shops for nail polish in town.

I take note of some of her favorite things—like yogurt-covered pretzels, pale peach lip gloss, and hooded sweatshirts with big front pockets.

And I know when she goes to bed, usually around eleven thirty, right after chatting online with I can only wonder who.

That's the hard part—not knowing EVERYTHING about her, despite how hard I try. Even when I'm up close, I can't always hear what she's saying in conversation. I can't always watch her lips, for fear she'll catch on, which would ruin everything.

I want to talk to her. And sometimes we do talk. But it's never for very long and we never say anything important.

I can't be myself around her. I can't relax or open up, or show her all the pictures I've got tacked up on my wall: pictures of her at the beach, in front of her house, at the mall, and in the bakery downtown.

Lately she's been talking to everyone, even to people she never normally associates with. She's been asking them questions about something that shouldn't even matter to her, something she shouldn't even know about.

Luckily, she redeemed herself, though. We got really close recently. Or, should I say, I got really close to her. At first I thought it made her nervous, but then it seemed like she kind of enjoyed it. Because she didn't back away.

I want to get close to her again. I want to see how far she'll let me go—how far I'll have to push before she has no choice but to let me in.

16

I T'S MONDAY AFTERNOON, the last block of the day, and a full six minutes and thirty seconds into chemistry class when Ben finally comes in.

He smiles at me, totally catching me off guard. And totally making my face heat up.

I saw him earlier today, too, and I had a similar reaction. We were passing one another near the front entranceway of the school when we collided, and his shoulder bumped against my forearm.

It nearly made me drop my books.

I mean, it wasn't *just* the mild collision. It was the way he lingered there, asking me if I was okay, telling me it was an accident, running his fingers over my arm to make sure I was okay. He gazed into my eyes and smiled an irresistible grin—as if we shared some secret.

My heart pounded, and my insides turned to bubbling

lava. I secretly hoped his bumping into me wasn't an accident at all, but 100 percent intentional.

Ben slides into the seat beside mine and starts flipping through his notes.

"Is everything okay, Ms. Hammond?" the Sweat-man asks, obviously noticing my spaceyness, and how I can't stop staring.

Ben looks beyond delicious, dressed in layers of chocolate brown. He glances at me, checking for my response, and so I give a quick nod, my insides stirring up even more.

Sweat-man continues with his lecture, failing to say anything about Ben's lateness, which only confirms the rumor that the principal's given Ben carte blanche as far as promptness goes. There are several theories as to why his tardiness is accepted. Some think it's for Ben's own safety—because he's constantly getting harassed, and maybe the administration is afraid a fight will break out in the hallway as people are changing classes. Others say it's because he has a phobia—either claustrophobia or agoraphobia, or possibly a blend of both.

Personally, I don't know the reason for his lag time. I'm just really happy to see him.

While Sweat-man prattles on—something about chemical and ionic bonding—I can't help noticing the olive tone of Ben's skin, the mole on his left cheek, and how every few minutes he turns to glance at me.

When class is finally over, he collects his books in a stack and then moves past me, the sleeve of his shirt brushing against my back, sending tingles all over my skin.

"I'll see you later," he says in a hushed tone.

I nod, wondering if he really means it, if he really intends to see me later, or if it's just his way of saying good-bye.

He heads up to talk to the Sweat-man, and I'm so tempted to hang around and wait until he's done.

But Kimmie spots me first. She pulls me from the doorway, yanks me out into the hall, all the while babbling on about how she needs to get to the mall—STAT—to buy herself some decent underwear.

"Sounds like a dire emergency," I say, keeping an eye on the chemistry room door.

"It *is* an emergency," she insists. "How can a girl this chic—meaning me, before you ask—run around with a rubber band holding up her undies?"

"Wait—*what?*"

"I have three words for you: underwear, broken elastic waistband, down around my ankles in Spanish class."

"Okay, but that was way more than three words."

"Whatever," she says. "Here, feel my ball." She gestures toward her waist.

"No, thanks." I grimace.

She smirks and shows me the ball of fabric bulging out from her vintage poodle skirt—where she's obviously got a rubber band tightened around her panty fabric to hold said panties up.

Meanwhile, I continue to keep focused on the door, anticipating Ben's exit.

"Did Kimmie tell you about Spanish?" Wes shouts, barreling his way up the hallway toward us.

Kimmie rolls her eyes. "Do we really need to rehash all the details?"

"Of course we do," he says. "Just picture it: it's before class, and Kimmie's on her way up to the front of the room to sharpen her pencil, not even realizing her underwear is falling down around her ankles. The next thing you know, Davis Miller grabs for it—"

"Okay, first of all," Kimmie interrupts, "let's just say there's been a lot of drama going on at my house as of late. A girl—even the most fashionably minded—doesn't always get it right, especially when she's racing out the door first thing in the morning for fear her dad might ask for another lesson on setting up a Ferrari blog. By the way, he wants everyone to call him Turbo from now on."

"And second of all?" Wes asks.

"Davis Miller is clearly the result of birth-control failure," she says. "He looks like a walking Mr. Potato Head with those bulging eyes, that bulbous nose, and those blubbery lips."

"But he does play a mean electric guitar. Have you heard his rendition of 'Walk This Way'? Seriously, it'll bring tears to your eyes." Wes uses the corner of his sleeve to dab at the invisible tears on his cheeks.

"Because it's so horrible?" Kimmie asks.

"Because it would make Steven Tyler proud."

"*Who?*" Her face scrunches up.

While the two continue to argue over what makes

great music, I keep an eye on the door, until I notice them staring at me, arms folded, awaiting my response.

"What?" I ask, feeling the color rise to my cheeks.

"My question exactly," Wes says. "What's up with you today?"

"Nothing." I sigh.

"Not nothing," he says. "You look like the old woman who swallowed a fly."

"*I guess she'll die,*" he and Kimmie sing in unison.

"Very funny." I laugh.

"No." Kimmie corrects me. "Funny would be Wes continuing to dress like a third grader on school-picture day. I mean, honestly. Dickies and boat shoes?" She tsk-tsks at his outfit. "Totally two decades ago."

"This from the girl who wears enough black eyeliner to paint a large hearse, casket included," Wes says.

"Not to mention granny panties," I add.

"Okay, minus the geriatric Skivvies, it's called style," Kimmie argues. "And we need to get Wes some, pronto. Camelia, are you in? Something tells me you could use some shopping therapy. Nothing like a fresh pair of undies to lift the spirits."

"That's what *I* always say," Wes says, girl-ifying his voice by raising it three octaves.

I nod somewhat reluctantly, warning her that I have to be back early for a tutoring session with Matt.

"Don't worry about it." She links arms with me. "We'll have you back in ample time to rendezvous with your ex."

We move quickly down the hallway, en route to our

lockers, Kimmie blabbering on about how she'll be forever remembered as the girl with the huge-ass granny panties.

Before we turn down the hallway to get to our lockers, I glance back one last time in the direction of the chemistry lab.

And that's when I see Ben, standing in the doorway, staring right back at me.

"Hold up," I say, stopping us in our tracks. "I think I forgot something."

"What did you forget?" Kimmie asks.

"Something," I say, pretending to search in my bag.

"Something, huh?" Kimmie looks in the direction of the chemistry lab.

Ben is still there.

"Something tall, dark, and dangerous, maybe?" She puts her hands on her hips. The poodle on her skirt glares at me, foaming at the mouth (a Kimmie-designed appliqué).

"Maybe." I shrug.

"And maybe you're too transparent."

"Like tissue paper," Wes adds.

"Well, Kimmie should know about tissue paper," I say, gesturing toward her stuffed bra. "I really think he wants to talk to me."

"So, then, why doesn't he come over here? Why is he just standing there, gawking at us?" Kimmie asks.

"The angoraphobia thing," Wes whispers, to remind her.

"That's *agora*phobia, you dumb-ass." She swats his

head with her rhinestone purse. "The poor boy doesn't have a fear of rabbit wool."

"Don't you think it's weird he's hanging around you all of a sudden?" Wes asks.

"He's not *hanging around me*," I snap.

"First, the parking lot," Kimmie begins. "Then you guys are conveniently paired up as lab partners."

"So he can poke you with his test tube," Wes chimes in.

"Right," Kimmie says. "And don't forget this morning in front of the school. We saw the way he rubbed up against you in the doorway."

"He didn't *rub up* against me," I bark. "We bumped into each other."

"Call it what you will," Wes says, "but that move would be considered illegal in some states."

"What, are you guys spying on me now?"

"Well, the mauling in lab class is public knowledge," Wes explains. "As for the doorway incident, Kimmie and I were on our way to say hi, but you and Ben the Butcher—that's what people are calling him, FYI—were looking a little too chummy for a party."

"And that was just in a doorway," Kimmie adds.

"Right," Wes continues. "Just imagine what could happen if we left you two alone in an entire foyer."

"Definitely peculiar," Kimmie says.

"Whatever," I say, refusing to get into it. I turn and head toward Ben.

But he's no longer anywhere in sight.

*A*FTER FINDING WES THE PERFECT non-third-grade school-picture-day outfit, complete with Adidas sneakers to replace his "two decades ago" boat shoes, and Abercrombie jeans in lieu of the Dickies, Kimmie and I drop him off at the arcade and make a plan to meet him at the food pavilion in a half hour.

Meanwhile, we make our way to the lingerie store.

"They can't just be *any* undies," Kimmie explains, picking through the pile of cotton briefs. "They have to call out to me. They have to say, 'I. Am. Worthy.' I mean, we are talking about my caboose here, right?"

"Right," I say, playing along, trying not to laugh out loud, even when she gives her caboose a shimmy-shake.

While Kimmie continues to look around, I decide to check out some pj's. I find a really cute pair—a snuggly pink hoodie top with matching fleece shorts. I hold them up to myself in the mirror.

"Too cute," Kimmie says, sneaking up behind me. "That's what you want to be wearing when the fire department rescues you in the middle of the night from the window of a blazing building."

"Exactly what I was thinking." I roll my eyes.

"So, I got the goods." She jiggles her shopping bag at me, having already paid.

"And did they call out to you?"

"These babies didn't just call; they screamed."

"Well, unfortunately, my wallet is screaming, too." I reluctantly return my pj's to the rack, and we head out to meet Wes, lingerie catalog—the price we're paying him for being our taxi this afternoon—in hand.

We end up making a couple more stops, including a trip to the drugstore for some self-tanner, which, according to Kimmie, is exactly what Wes's "pale-ass" complexion could use.

"You'll be stylin' in no time," she tells him.

"I'd better be," he says. "Because if I don't start bringing some girls home soon, my dad's gonna sign me up for Girl Scouts. No joke. He's already threatened it twice."

"Well your dad's a psycho," Kimmie says.

"A psycho who wants his son to be a stud, maybe. Did I ever mention he got voted Best Looking and Most Datable in high school?"

"About a thousand times," she drones.

"He expects me to be just like him," he continues.

"Furry, fat, and bald?" she asks. "Honestly, try the self-tanner. Then we'll work on getting you a date."

When I arrive home, Matt is already waiting at the dining room table for our study session.

"Am I late?" I ask, checking my watch. It's barely six thirty.

He shakes his head. "Your mom let me in. I just thought we'd get a head start."

"Didn't you have a date earlier?"

He nods and flips a page in his book, snacking from a bowlful of what appears to be soy butter–drizzled popcorn, my mother's signature snack.

And so, before I can even say, *"parlez-vous* pain-in-the-butt?" we get right down to it, our elbows deep in *la grammaire fantastique.*

"It just doesn't make any sense." Matt sighs.

"Why don't we move on to vocab?" I suggest, after a good hour and a half of phrase-and-clause hell.

Matt agrees, and we spend the next half hour going over *la liste.* "I think you're ready," I say, slamming his book shut.

"I don't." He lets out another sigh.

"Quick, how do you say 'movie star'?"

"Cinéphile?"

"No." I flick a popcorn kernel at his forehead. "A *cinéphile* is a person who frequents the movies. A *vedette* is a movie star."

"Right." He nods.

"Speaking of movies," I segue, "how was your hot date with Rena this afternoon? Did she do that hyena giggling thing?" Last year in gym class, she practically had to get mouth-to-mouth from laughing so hard at Mr. Muse in his spandex biker shorts.

"Do I detect an air of jealousy?"

"What you detect is mere curiosity," I say, correcting him.

"How do *you* think it went?" He glances at my mouth as I chew.

"I don't know," I say, remembering how Kimmie said she didn't believe they were dating at all. "You're eating my mom's popcorn, aren't you?"

"And what does that have to do with anything?"

"Who eats the soy-buttered organic blend after going to the movies, where there's tubfuls of the good stuff? Not to mention the fact that you were here early. . . ."

"So?"

"So my guess is that you didn't even go. Am I right?"

"Nope," he says with a smirk. "Rena and I caught an early show and feasted on gummy worms and nacho chips. But I'll give you an A for effort."

"I guess there's no kissing and telling with you, huh?"

"I think your parentals do enough kissing for the both of us." He gestures to the sofa in the next room, where my mom and dad are snuggled up. Dad is stroking my mom's hair and nuzzling her neck, but my mom has this faraway stare, like she's someplace else entirely.

"Seriously, could my parents be any more mortifying?" I ask, trying to keep things light.

"Your dad's a lucky guy."

For environmental reasons, they only had one child—me—but at the rate they were going, I'm guessing they could have had dozens.

"Remember when we caught them making out in the backseat of your mom's SUV?" he continues.

"My parents have this philosophy that Americans are way too reserved. And so they feel a social responsibility to display themselves pawing all over each other whenever the occasion arises—to cure America of its prudishness."

"Makes sense to me." He smiles and wipes a stray piece of popcorn from my cheek.

"Very glamorous," I joke, grabbing a napkin.

He smiles a little more broadly. His teal blue eyes match his shirt.

"Want to watch TV?" I suggest, suddenly sensing a bit of awkwardness between us.

"Actually, I should probably get going."

"Are you sure?" I ask, almost reluctant to see him leave.

He nods and fishes through the side pocket of his backpack. "Before I forget, I have something to show you." He pulls forth not one, but two article clippings that detail the events of the so-called murder that Ben was allegedly involved in. "I told you I'd get the scoop."

"Wait—where did you get these?"

"First, answer my question. Is it true about what happened in lab—did he really grab you?"

"It was nothing," I say, anxiously perusing the articles.

Both of them basically state that two minors, a male and a female, both age fifteen, went on a hiking trip one day, two years ago, and that the girl fell from a cliff and died instantly. "So, it was an accident."

Matt shrugs. "I hear there's a lot more to it."

"Like what?" I ask, noticing there are no names listed in the articles. "And how do you even know it's him?"

"Like I said, I've been hearing stuff."

"Hearing from who?"

"*Whom,* not who," he says, to be funny. "I may suck at French, but I'm good in English."

"*And?*"

"And I don't know." He shrugs again. "Mrs. Shelley, Principal Snell's secretary, has a friend who lives in the town where it happened. That's how all the details leaked out in the first place."

"What details?"

"That Ben pushed her, that he has a history of violence. And that this wouldn't have been the first time he laid his hands on her."

"He laid his hands on her?" I repeat, the words getting caught in my throat.

"I don't know," Matt repeats. "That's just what I heard."

"So, why isn't he in jail?"

He shakes his head. "He was arrested, and there was a trial, but there were no witnesses, and they didn't have enough proof."

"Even with a history of violence?"

Matt shrugs. "I know. It doesn't make sense, which is why everyone was pissed about the outcome. They thought he was guilty."

"But the judge and jury didn't?"

"Not that it mattered. Ben got so ridiculed after the trial that he ended up dropping out of school. What he's doing here is beyond me."

I sink back in my seat, feeling a knot form in my gut.

"Are you okay?" He reaches out to touch my arm.

I nod and look away.

"Just keep your distance," Matt continues, his eyes full of concern.

"He's my lab partner, remember?"

"So, can't you ask to switch?"

"Don't worry," I say, getting up from the table. "I won't let him lay a hand on me." And just as the words escape my lips, I can't help noticing the irony of it all— since it was just a couple of days ago, when Ben clasped my wrist and made my heart swell, that I didn't want him to ever let go.

18

I<small>T'S TUESDAY MORNING</small>, just before the first bell, and I'm sitting outside on one of the benches that overlook the Tree-Hugger Society's prize-winning garden, eating the remainder of the whole-grain granola bar that my mother insisted I take with me this morning.

A bunch of people pass by me on their way inside and, though I've resolved to put the whole photo issue out of my mind, I can't help wondering who the jokester is, and whether he or she might be lurking somewhere now, camera in hand.

John Kenneally, Kimmie's flavor of the week, waves to me as he drives around to the parking lot behind the school. And so does Kimmie herself, her 1920s flapper boa flailing out the window of Wes's car.

With only two bites left, I hear it—him. Ben's motorcycle pulls into the traffic circle with a rumble. But, instead of driving past me, he stops, removes his helmet, and raises his hand to wave.

"What are you doing out here?" he asks, approaching me.

I flash him my granola bar. "Just having a little breakfast before the bell rings. Want a bite?"

He shakes his head. "I was actually hoping we could talk."

"Sure," I say, thinking back to everything Matt told me last night, and suddenly feeling a slight twinge in my stomach.

Ben sits down beside me on the bench.

"Is everything okay?" I ask, trying to sound calm.

He nods and looks off toward the garden. "I just wanted to say, sorry about what happened the other day in chemistry."

"Did you get in trouble?"

He shrugs. "Detention for a week, starting tomorrow."

"That seems harsh."

"Everything at this school seems harsh."

I bite my lip, unsurprised by his perception of this tiny-town place.

"So, I suppose you've heard some stuff about me," he continues.

"A little."

"Care to elaborate?"

I shrug and follow his gaze, still focused on the garden. "Why don't you tell me?"

"Maybe another time," he says, finally turning to look at me. "I just thought, since we have to work together and all, we should probably start over."

"What do you mean?"

He gazes at my hair, noticing maybe how I've got it pulled into two artfully messed-up braids. "You know, like we never met."

"Like you never saved my life?"

He smiles slightly; the corners of his pale pink lips curl up. "Something like that," he says, staring at my mouth now.

"So, you're admitting it?"

He smirks, angling his body toward me more. He smells like maple sugar mixed with motorcycle fumes. "I admit to nothing."

"So, what *did* happen the other day . . . in chemistry class?"

"I accidentally dropped the test tube."

"No, I mean just after that . . . when you touched me—when you grabbed my wrist."

"It was just an accident."

"That was no accident."

"It was." He looks away again.

"Are you sure there's nothing you want to tell me?"

Ben shakes his head and I purse my lips, wondering why he insists on keeping all these secrets, when he's obviously trying to clear things up.

"So, shall we start over?" he asks.

"I guess," I say, still utterly confused.

"Hi, my name's Ben Carter." He smiles, fully aware of how cheesy this is.

"Camelia Hammond." I grin. "And before you ask, yes,

it's true, my parents are hippies and thought it'd be fun to name me after a lizard. I changed the spelling, against their wishes."

"Well, I guess that means you have good survival instincts," he says, edging in a little closer. "You must adapt well to your surroundings."

"Oh my god, you sound *exactly* like my mother."

"I'll try and forget you said that." He smiles wider. "So, do you get out much, Camelia Hammond?"

"Like, for good behavior?"

"Like, on dates. What do you say? Are you free Saturday?"

I take a deep breath and mutter the word *no*. Only it comes out as *yes*.

"Great," he says. "How about around two? We can meet for a late lunch."

I nod, and he gets up, bumping his knee against mine in the process.

"Are you okay?" I ask, noticing how upset he suddenly looks. His eyes narrow, and he takes a step back.

"I gotta go," he says, refusing to look me in the eye.

"What is it?" I ask, standing up, too.

But instead of answering, he heads back to his motorcycle and speeds away—just as fast as he did on the day that he saved my life.

19

She was out in front of school this morning, looking for attention. Like a total slut.

The front of school is her new place to be noticed. Nobody else ever just hangs out there, but she wants to be on display, so people look at her as soon as they pull up.

I said the alphabet forwards and backwards and counted up building bricks to keep myself calm. It was either that or haul off and smack her stupid little face.

She just makes me so mad sometimes, so mad that I can't quite think straight. She wants to see me lose control.

20

*B*EN AND I HAVE ARRANGED TO MEET at Seaview
Park for our date. He'd wanted to pick me up, but
Kimmie insisted on tagging along.

"I know the rumors aren't true," she says, "but if anything weird ever happened and I didn't do anything to try
and stop it, I'd never be able to forgive myself."

"Anything weird?"

She shrugs. "Like if you wound up tied up, dead, and
buried in a shallow grave somewhere."

"Seriously?"

"Kidding." She rolls her eyes. "But that still doesn't change
the fact that Mr. Touchy-Feely completely creeps me out."

I watch as she sifts through my bedroom closet for
something for me to wear, wondering if I'm doing the
right thing. I mean, yes, I want to find out the truth about
him, but I honestly can't remember a time when I've been
more unnerved.

"How about this one?" she asks, holding up a lavender tunic.

I take it and slip it on, too rattled even to pay much attention.

"The winner," she announces, tossing me a pair of leggings and my strappy sandals.

Originally the plan was that she and Wes would come and we'd make it a foursome, but unfortunately, that plan got snagged when Kimmie was grounded for making her eight-year-old brother, Nate, do all her household chores for a week. As punishment, Kimmie's parents have declared her Nate's own personal slave for a period of seventy-two hours. Kimmie has spent the last twenty-four of those hours dodging water balloons, making grilled-cheese-and-gummy-worm sandwiches, playing hide-and-seek, and organizing her brother's Matchbox car collection according to type, color, size, and year.

You'd think all that torture would suffice. But not quite. Nate refuses to let Kimmie have the afternoon off.

"He says either he comes along, or I can't go."

"Are you kidding?" I ask, pulling the leggings on.

"Not kidding. I tried to talk him out of it, but that just made him want to come more. I'm lucky he even gave me this hour off for good behavior. You look hot, by the way."

"Thanks," I say, running my fingers through my kinky hair, and seriously wondering if I'm going to be sick.

"Don't worry," Kimmie assures me. "You won't even know we're there."

"Right," I say, fairly confident that that won't be the case.

But we go anyway—Kimmie and me in the front seat of her parents' minivan and Nate in the back, armed with his basketball, baseball, and hockey equipment. We pull into the parking lot, my eyes scanning the area, looking for Ben by the pavilion, at the fountain, or on one of the park benches.

I finally spot him sitting on a blanket in the distance, a basket and cooler set up in front of him.

"Who knew Ben the Butcher was such a romantic?" Kimmie whips a pair of binoculars out of her purse for a better view.

I take a deep breath, trying to calm my jangled nerves. Meanwhile, Kimmie adjusts the zoom lens on her binoculars, zeroing in on a guy jogging in the distance.

"Hey, that totally looks like your boss. Does Spencer run?"

"Okay, can we just focus on me for a moment?"

"Relax. I'll only be a slasher-movie scream away," she teases.

"At the baseball diamond," Nate specifies. He pulls on his catcher's mask.

Kimmie gives me a quick hug for luck, and then I climb out of the van and make my way toward Ben. But, before I can even get halfway there, a soccer ball comes flying in my direction.

"Heads up!" I hear somebody yell.

I stop the ball using the heel of my sandal, and then

look up in search of the owner. It's John Kenneally. He comes running to retrieve it.

"Thanks," he says, catching my throw. "Ever think about trying out for goalie?"

I smile and glance over his shoulder, where it appears his soccer team is having a scrimmage.

"Seems we've been bumping into each other a lot lately," he says.

I nod and scan the park for Kimmie, surprised she didn't spot John right away, especially with her binoculars. "Do you guys always practice here on Saturdays?"

He nods. "Usually from one to three, just after lunch."

"Great," I say, filing the information away so I can share it with Kimmie later.

"Really?"

I nod again, trying not to act too enthusiastic, even though I've probably already overdone it.

While John heads back to his teammates, I head in Ben's direction. It appears as though he's already spotted me.

"Hey!" he shouts, waving me over.

He couldn't look more amazing—hair messed up to perfection; torn jeans; and a crewneck sweater that clings just enough to his chest.

We sit, and he pops the cork off a bottle of faux champagne. "I'm really glad you came."

"Did you think I wouldn't?"

He shrugs and pours me a glass.

"Thanks," I say, taking a sip.

Ben unloads the basket. He's got a whole spread

prepared for us, including a loaf of honey bread, thick wedges of sharp cheddar cheese, and an antipasto with olives, marinated peppers, and eggplant.

"This looks incredible," I say.

"Wait till you see what I've got for dessert."

We end up talking about everything: about how he practices meditation and takes tae kwon do, and how I've been sculpting clay since before I could even throw a ball.

"You start with this shapeless mound," I tell him, "and what you make from it is totally up to you. You're in complete control of what it becomes."

"But what if it doesn't turn out the way you want?"

"Start fresh," I say, tearing off a hunk of honey bread.

"And ditch the other piece?"

"Why not?"

"I don't know." He shrugs. "Sometimes I think it's good to be open to the stuff that doesn't seem to work. Sometimes that's the best stuff."

"Are you a sculptor, too?"

"Not since Play-Doh." He smiles. "But I like to write sometimes."

"Poetry?"

"Song lyrics."

"Have you ever been in a band?"

He shakes his head. "It's a little hard when you're being homeschooled—a little hard to meet people."

"How long were you homeschooled?"

"A couple years. Technically, I should be a senior, but I got behind, which is why my schedule's all screwed up.

Did you know I'm taking some freshman classes?"

I shake my head, surprised there's a tidbit of gossip I haven't heard yet.

"Anyway," he continues, "when my aunt asked if I wanted to live here with her—two hours away from my hometown—so I could go to public school again, I said yes."

"So you *could* go to public school?"

"As you can probably guess, when you have a rep like mine, public school is sort of a drag."

I nod, remembering what Matt said—how after the trial Ben got ridiculed so badly he had to drop out of school. I'm tempted to ask him more, but before I can, he tells me he'd love to learn sculpture one day and it'd be great if I could teach him.

We hang out for another couple of hours—through full-on Nate-and-Kimmie matches of basketball and baseball and a tire-swing competition—eating up the rest of the picnic lunch as well as the makeshift s'more dessert he made using oatmeal cookies, chocolate fudge sauce, and marshmallow spread.

"You'll never go back to the old campfire style," he says, handing me one.

I take a bite and a long, embarrassing moan escapes my mouth before I can stop it.

"That good, huh?"

"Better than good." I finish it off.

"You're really great, you know that?"

I smile, totally caught off guard. I try to think up

something clever to say back, but instead I just tell him, "You're pretty great, too."

Ben wipes some chocolate from my lips with his napkin. "I'm really glad we did this."

"Yeah," I say. "Me, too."

"So, does that mean you want to do it again?"

My face grows warm, and my lip trembles slightly.

Ben moves in a little closer. And then I do something totally out of the ordinary for me—something I didn't plan.

I kiss him.

My mouth presses against his, and he kisses me back, sending tingles all over my skin.

I start to draw him in closer—to run my fingers down his back. But he pulls away, and our lips make an unpleasant smacking sound.

Then he stands up. He tells me we'd better get going and then starts putting away all the empty food containers.

"Wait! What just happened?" I ask.

Ben doesn't answer. He just folds up the blanket and tosses it over his shoulder. Grabs the basket and takes off, without any explanation. Without so much as a good-bye.

21

*I*NSTEAD OF DROPPING ME OFF right away, Kimmie cruises around—with her brother's approval, thanks to some edible incentive via Mickey D's drive-through, so that I can give her the full report.

"Well, I can't say I'm not relieved," she says of the disastrous end to my date. "I mean, when I said I wanted you to get out more, I didn't expect you to pick the creepiest boy of the bunch."

"Whatever." I sigh.

"At least nothing super-icky happened when you kissed him." She proceeds to remind me how in the eighth grade she threw up on Buddy McTeague when he insisted on kissing her, even though she'd warned him she had the stomach flu.

"No, nothing icky," I assure her. "The kiss was amazing—at least it started out that way."

"Details, please."

I close my eyes, my lips still buzzing from his kiss.

"Were there a bunch of little kisses that led up to one great big giant fat one?" she continues. "Or did he just go in with tongue from the get-go? Was there superfluous slurpage? Distracting sucking sounds? Weird or unpleasant odor? Exchange of food bits or drink? Did your tongues swirl in sync, or just kind of bump into each other?"

"Whoa," I say, putting a halt to her list. "Let's just say it started out well, but ended sort of sucky."

"No pun intended."

"I'm such an idiot." I sigh.

"No, 'idiot' would be me," she says, feeding another Scooby-Doo CD into the player.

I take a peek at the backseat, where Nate is bouncing up and down in anticipation of Scooby *Snack Tracks* #1.

We end up driving around a bit more, until just before seven, when she finally drops me off with a promise to call me later.

I wave good-bye to her and make my way up the front steps, noticing how the streetlight in front of my house has gone out, leaving the area in near darkness.

Just a few steps shy of the door, I hear something behind me—a scuffling sound. I turn to look, but I can't see too much in the dark, and the sound seems to have stopped now. The only thing I can hear is the noise coming out of Davis Miller's garage-turned-music-studio down the street.

I turn back around to open the front door when I hear the scuffling again, like footsteps against the pavement.

Like someone's coming this way.

"Kimmie?" I call out. I strain to see, wondering if I left something in her car.

But no one answers, and I don't see her car anywhere.

I fish inside my pocket for my key ring and finally find the house key among the collection I've got going. I go to stick it in the lock, but the ring falls from my grip, landing on the welcome mat.

I take a deep breath, trying to stay calm. I kneel to pick up my keys, but can't keep my hands from shaking. I decide to ring the doorbell, knowing that my parents are probably home. But before I can actually reach up to press it, someone touches my shoulder, making me jump.

"Ben," I say, completely startled to see him.

"I'm sorry I scared you." He takes a step back.

"What are you doing here? How do you even know where I live?" I glance over his shoulder, but I don't see his motorcycle.

"I looked you up in the phone book. I hope that's okay."

"So why didn't you call?"

"I wanted to talk face to face," he says, venturing a little closer. "I wanted to tell you that I'm sorry about earlier."

"Don't worry about it," I snap, moving toward the door again.

"No—wait." He takes another step. "Can we talk?"

Part of me wants to tell him no—that this whole scenario is just a little too weird. I glance up at the porch light, wondering why my parents didn't turn it on.

"Please," he insists. "It'll only take a couple of minutes."

I hesitate, but then notice his troubled look, as if he

really does need to tell me something important. "Okay," I say, hoping I won't regret it.

I sit on the top step. Ben sits beside me and stares up at the moon. "I meant it when I said that I think you're pretty great," he says.

"Well, then, why all the mixed messages?"

"There is a good reason."

"Which is?"

"I didn't mean to scare you," he repeats. "And what I'm going to say . . . I don't want that to scare you, either."

"What are you talking about?" I peek toward the driveway at my parents' car, relieved to know for sure they're home.

"It was me."

"What was you?"

"In the parking lot . . . behind the school. It was me who pushed you out of the way when that car was coming toward you."

"And why are you finally admitting this now?"

"Because you're in danger," he says, his eyes wide and intense.

"Excuse me?"

"It sounds crazy, but it's true."

"And how do you know this?"

"I can't tell you, and I realize it's a lot to ask, but you have to trust me."

"I don't even know you, really."

"Exactly. Which makes this all the more difficult."

"I'm not in danger," I assure him.

"You are," he says, tensing his jaw. "At first I didn't want to believe it, either, but after today, I'm sure of it."

"After today?"

He looks back toward the moon. "Just think about it. Has anything weird or unusual happened lately? Is there anyone around you that you don't trust?"

"Wait—did you hear something? At school? Is there something that I should know?"

He shakes his head. "It isn't anything like that."

"Then what?"

"You're in danger," he says again. "But I want to help you."

I shake my head, my mind hazy with questions. "I think I should probably go in. My parents are probably wondering where I am."

He nods and studies my face, his gaze lingering on my mouth. "Just think about what I said. And know that I'm here if you want to talk. You can call me anytime—day or night."

"Thanks," I whisper, not knowing what else to say, or if I should even say anything at all.

Ben nods and walks away. I watch him go until he's swallowed up by the darkness. A few seconds later, I hear his motorcycle rev and take off.

Instead of going inside, I sit for several more minutes on the front steps, wondering what just happened. And what it means.

It just seems so weird—that I'm supposedly in danger. So weird, because his girlfriend was in danger, too.

22

I<small>T'S ALMOST SEVEN THIRTY</small> when I finally go inside. "Hey, sweetie," my mom calls out. "Dinner's not for another half hour. Soma noodle surprise with tempeh chunks and zucchini-prune juice."

As if that's supposed to tempt me.

I head into the kitchen to see if she needs any help, but she and my dad are in the living room, doing partners yoga. My mom's lying on the floor in front of my dad, whom she's got knotted up in the lotus position. Her feet are elevated and locked around his neck. "Care to join us?" she asks. "This is wonderful for digestion."

My mom's family album—the one she normally keeps locked up in the cedar chest—is sitting out on the coffee table. It's open to the picture of Mom and Aunt Alexia when they were kids, posing by the Christmas tree.

"I'm not really hungry," I say, wondering what's going on, if Aunt Alexia is in some kind of trouble again.

My dad, a conservative tax attorney by day and my mom's yoga victim by night, gives me a pleading look. But, unfortunately for him, my downward-facing-dog days ended around the age of twelve, when my mom paid a visit to my class on career day and talked about the benefits of colon cleansing.

"Matt called for you again," she says, her voice rising above the Buddhist monk's chant coming from our stereo.

"What do you mean, *again?*"

"He called yesterday, but maybe I forgot to tell you."

"Is it something important?"

"He didn't say." She plunges her heels into my poor dad's shoulders in an effort to arch herself upward. "Someone else called for you today, too."

"Someone else?"

"He wouldn't leave a name."

"He?"

She manages a nod in spite of the position she's in. "When I told him you weren't home, he hung up before I could say anything else. How was your date, by the way?"

"Interesting," I say, thinking about Ben—about how when I asked him why he didn't call me instead of just coming over, he said he wanted to talk face to face. "Did whoever it was say he'd call back?"

But my mother, having finally gotten into her backbend, is too busy counting kundalini breaths to answer me now. And so I head up to my room, wondering if I should get Kimmie's take on all this. I reach for the phone, but it rings before I can even pick it up.

"Hello?"

"Hello, Camelia," says a male voice.

"Who's this?"

"Who do you think it is?"

"Ben?" I ask, my heart pumping hard.

He doesn't answer.

"Okay, I'm going to hang up," I say.

"Maybe we should talk first," the voice whispers.

"Not if you don't tell me who you are."

"You're so pretty; you know that?"

I click the phone off so I can dial *69, but I don't get a dial tone.

Because we're still connected.

"You think hanging up on me will make me go away?" he asks.

I hang up again and the phone rings, not two seconds later. I click it on, but I don't say a word.

"I know you're there," he says.

"Who is this?"

"You can hang up on me all you want, but you can't get away. I'm everywhere you are—watching you, dreaming about you—"

"Wes?" I ask, hoping it's him and that this is another one of his lame jokes.

"Consider this your warning," he says. His voice is smooth and deep.

"My warning for what?"

"For being a good girl. Will you be a good girl for me?"

My mouth opens, but nothing comes out. I click the phone back off. This time it disconnects, and I'm able to dial *69. But the caller's number is blocked.

"Camelia," my mother calls.

I take a deep breath, trying to get a grip, wondering what he meant about how he's everywhere I am.

I leave the phone off the hook so he can't call back, and then glance toward my bedroom windows. A breeze blows the curtains into the room.

I know for a fact that I didn't leave my windows open this morning.

Slowly I move toward them, wondering if maybe my mom was trying to air out the room. In one quick motion I pull the curtains open completely, steeling myself for whatever happens next.

But there's nothing out there—nothing unusual, that is. A cluster of trees, my dad's toolshed, and Mr. Ludinsky's minivan, parked in front of our house.

I let out a breath and look again, noticing that both the windowpane and the screen are hiked up at least six inches. Did my mom or dad do this? Even though neither ever comes into my bedroom. Did *I* do this? Is there something I'm not remembering? I glance around my room, but everything appears just as neat and orderly as I left it. Meanwhile, my mind is spinning, and my hands won't stop shaking.

I move to close the window again. That's when I see a pink package, sitting in the flower box.

I grab it, still telling myself this must be some stupid joke. Aside from a pink bow that sits on top, the package is blank—no name, no card—and so I wonder if it's even for me.

"Camelia," my mother calls again.

"In a second," I say, tearing the paper off. I recognize the pink and green packaging right away. It's a gift box from the lingerie store.

I close my eyes, still able to hear the caller's voice in my ear, telling me that he's watching me.

Was he watching me at the mall the other day?

I lift the cover off the box and unfold the contents from the layers of tissue, the answer becoming quickly apparent.

It's the pink pj's that I picked from the rack at the store and then put back. A note sticks out of the pocket. With trembling fingers, I open it. The words *THIS IS OUR LITTLE SECRET* are scribbled across the page in bright red marker.

I drop the note and cover my mouth, trying my best to hold it all together.

A moment later, I feel something touch my back. I whirl around and let out a gasp.

"Camelia?" Dad asks, standing right behind me.

"You startled me," I say, closing the box back up.

"Didn't you hear your mother? Dinner's ready." He rolls his shoulders back with a crack.

"Were you in my room today?" I ask, glancing toward my window.

He shakes his head.

"Was Mom?"

"Not that I know of, why?"

I shrug, too embarrassed to explain to my dad that

someone left me a gift from a lingerie store.

"Are you sure everything's all right?" he asks.

I nod, somehow mustering a smile.

"So how come the phone's off the hook?" he asks, pushing for information.

"Oh," I say, just noticing it, even though the dial tone blares like a siren between us. "Wes thinks it's funny to prank me."

"But he wasn't the one who called you earlier," he says; it's more of a statement than a question.

"No. I mean, I don't know. I don't think so."

"Camelia?" he asks, reaching out to touch my shoulder.

I'm just about to cave completely when he says, "Dinner's on the table. Get the tempeh while it's still chewable."

"I'm not really hungry."

"Well, come anyway. It'll make Mom happy. She's been a little blue lately."

"Why, what's going on?"

"Nothing really—just some stuff with her sister. She's convinced herself something isn't right with her." He twists his hips, producing more cracks. "We can talk more after dinner—catch up on stuff. I'll make us some hot chocolate. The real kind, with cream and sugar. No soy products whatsoever."

"Sounds good," I say, hoping I'm doing the right thing by not telling him what happened.

Not yet at least.

INSTEAD OF FATHER-DAUGHTER CHATTING with Dad after dinner, I tell him that Kimmie's in crisis mode and wants me to come over, pronto. Luckily my parents don't give me a hard time, which only makes me feel worse. I honestly hate having to lie to them like this. To compound the guilt, Mom even packs me up a care package, complete with granola-flaxseed bars and carob-walnut cookies (it's the thought that counts), and then drops me off in front of Kimmie's house.

Kimmie is one big question mark when I show up on her doorstep—one big *green* question mark, I should say. There's a thick layer of olive green mud mask on her face and, oddly enough, she's wearing a pair of matching green footie pajamas—whether to coordinate or by coincidence, I have no idea.

"Did your mom tell you I was coming?" I ask, noticing Nate camped out on the stairs to eavesdrop, a notepad and a pencil in his hands.

She shakes her head, her wet hair swept up in a towel.

"Well, I needed to talk, and I told your mom it was an emergency. You were in the shower."

"Say no more." She grabs me by the arm and ushers me past Nate.

We head up to her bedroom, and she closes the door behind us. "So, what's up?" She takes a seat on the corner of her bed.

"Something really weird is going on," I say, plunking down beside her.

"Weird as in John Kenneally asking you for my number? Of course, that probably wouldn't be too weird, would it? The boy did lend me a brand-new, sharpened, number two pencil in English yesterday."

"Can we please forget about John Kenneally for five measly minutes?"

Kimmie's mouth drops open, as if the idea of it appalls her.

"Did you notice anyone following us at the mall the other day?" I continue.

"No, why?" She furrows her eyebrows, creating cracks in the mud mask.

I pull the pajamas from my backpack.

"Wait, are those granola bars?" Kimmie spots the Tupperware containers Mom packed in my bag.

"Focus," I say, showing her the gift-packaging. "This is the same outfit I picked out at the store. Someone left it outside my bedroom window."

"*Someone*, or Wes?"

"Why would Wes buy this for me?"

Kimmie shrugs, inspecting a granola bar. "His family has way more money than they know what to do with—hence Wes's staggering allowance. Maybe he was trying to be nice. Are these hazelnuts?"

"Then, why not just offer to buy it for me?" I ask. "Why leave it outside my window?"

"Maybe he has a crush on you and wants to be all mysterious."

"That's doubtful."

"It's possible," she says, correcting me.

"It wasn't you, right?"

"I'm not *that* generous," she says, looking at the seventy-dollar price tag.

"There's more," I say, taking a deep breath. I pull the note from my pocket and hand it to her.

"*This is our little secret,*" she reads.

"Do you think it's a threat?"

Kimmie's mud-slathered face goes blank, like she doesn't know what to say.

"Some guy called me tonight, too," I tell her. "He said he's watching me. He said he's everywhere I am."

"Wait—*what*?"

"It's true." Hearing myself say this all out loud makes me feel even more freaked out.

"Did he say he left something outside your window?"

I shake my head.

"Okay, so slow down. There's no need to assume that

whoever pranked you today is the same person who left this stuff outside your window."

"Why *wouldn't* I assume it? Have you forgotten about the photograph in my mailbox?"

"A joke," she reminds me. "For all you know, this could be two different people—a jokester and an admirer."

"Or a psycho and a psycho-er."

Kimmie laughs. "That totally sounds like something I would say."

"Kimmie, somebody's following me. He said his phone call was to warn me."

"About what?"

"To be a good girl." My voice is shaky. "For all I know, he's been inside my bedroom."

"Okay, let's not get all paranoid. We'll call Wes. We'll find out if he's behind any of this. Are you sure the guy who called didn't sound even a *little* like him? The boy's got more voices than I've got vintage handbags."

"Wait," I say, letting out a breath. "It gets weirder. Ben said I was in danger."

"And why am I only hearing about this now?"

I tell her everything—how he showed up at my house tonight, and how he finally admitted to pushing me out of the way in the parking lot behind the school, and how he said I was in danger.

"Um, hello, so *there's* your answer." She pretends to knock at my head. "Creepy boy who watches you from afar, then shows up at your house shortly before he calls you . . ."

"Yes, but if he's the one who's doing all this, why

would he warn me I'm in danger? Why would he show up at my house on the same day I get a bizarre phone call and a mysterious gift left in the flower box outside my window?"

"I don't know. Maybe to keep you guessing—so you don't suspect him."

"He said that at first he didn't want to believe I was in danger—but now, after today, he's sure of it."

"So, what happened between your date and when he showed up at your house?"

"Or, maybe the better question is what happened *on* my date. I mean, things were going perfectly fine until I kissed him."

"What does kissing him have to do with you being in danger? Does he have a killer case of herpes or something?"

"He said he wanted to help me," I continue. "He gave me his phone number and said I could call him."

"And did you?"

I shake my head. "I was tempted to, but then, I don't know. I called you instead."

"Wise choice." Kimmie pulls the towel from her hair and fingers the jet black layers. "This is probably just some scheme he's got going to get close to you."

"But then why pull away when I kiss him?"

"Cold sores?"

"I'm serious."

"So am I," she says. "Ever have one? They're a bitch."

"Maybe I should call him."

"Him as in Ben? No way."

"What happened to innocent until proven guilty?" I ask.

"That was Wes's T-shirt. Mine says, 'Killers suck and they belong behind bars, not dating my best friend.'"

"I thought you didn't believe the rumors."

Before she can respond, there's a knock on her door.

"Who is it?" Kimmie shouts.

No one answers.

She rolls her eyes and gets up to open it.

It's Nate. He falls into the room with a thud, having been leaning up against the door, listening in on our every word.

"You're such a lame little loser!" Kimmie shouts, ripping the notepad from his clutches. She tears the pages out and flushes them down the toilet in the bathroom across the hall. "Kiss it good-bye, Encyclopedia Brown!"

Nate lets out a scream, gaining the attention of Kimmie's parents, her older sister, and her grandmother, who lives in the downstairs apartment. Even the dog starts barking at all the commotion.

Definitely my cue to leave.

24

I hate seeing her with other guys. The way she flirts with them and laughs at their stupid jokes.

I saw her talking to that dirtbag. So I called her. I had to set things straight. To put her in her place. And to warn her.

She needs to KNOW I'm not going anywhere.

Then maybe she'll think twice before she tries to make me jealous.

25

UNABLE TO REACH WES OVER the weekend, I track him down first thing Monday morning to ask if he had anything to do either with calling me Saturday or with the gift left outside my window.

"How would that be possible?" He drapes his camera strap over his shoulder, en route to the photo studio. "I wasn't even with you guys when you went to the undies store. How would I know which pajama set you picked out?"

"Any chance you were spying on us in the store?"

He lets out a laugh, but then realizes I'm not joking.

"I know. It's stupid," I continue.

"Of course, the proof is in the pj's," he jokes.

"And obviously someone *was* spying on me."

"It wasn't this someone." He slams his locker door shut. "I don't even know your size."

"And you didn't call me Saturday?"

"Not that I can remember," he says, tapping his finger against his bright orange chin—victim of the self-tanner. The poor boy looks like the Sunkist factory exploded on his face. "However, I could be bribed to rethink it with, say, a week's worth of English homework."

"Be serious."

"Take it or leave it."

"Do you know something?"

"Do you have the answers to the *Macbeth* questions?"

"Don't be a jerk."

"*Me*? Did you not just accuse me of spying on you, prank-calling you, and trespassing on your property? Not to mention buying you skeevy lingerie?"

"It wasn't skeevy," I say.

"Well, that figures." Wes fakes a yawn. "Bottom line, I'm not the one dating a murderer, remember? So, why don't you go bark up his guilty ass?" He attempts to brush pass me, but I'm able to stop him by grabbing the sleeve of his brand-new, Kimmie-selected, Abercrombie shirt.

"Don't be mad," I say. "I was actually hoping it was you."

"You were?" He raises an eyebrow.

"Well, yeah," I say, remembering what Kimmie said about him possibly having a crush on me. "I mean, I'd obviously rather it be you than some wacko."

"There's a compliment if I ever heard one."

"That's not what I meant," I say, suddenly hating the sound of my own voice.

But, instead of indulging me in even one more

syllable, he pulls away and heads off to homeroom.

Great.

In pottery class, Kimmie is all abuzz, telling me how she heard—but can't confirm—that Spencer is the substitute for today. "And we didn't even need to give Ms. Mazur whooping cough," she says.

"Right," I say, playing along.

Not even thirty seconds later, the rumor's confirmed. Spencer walks in, grabs a dry-erase marker, and writes his name on the board, explaining that Ms. Mazur is out for some professional development thing.

"Will she be out tomorrow, too?" Kimmie asks.

"Nope," Spencer says. "Now, let's get to work."

"So much for small talk," Kimmie coughs out, adding a coil to her clay pot.

I'm making a coil pot, too—one with a bubblelike base and a twisted handle.

Just as Ms. Mazur always does, Spencer takes a trip around the room, making comments and suggestions about everybody's work.

"What do you think?" Kimmie asks once he reaches us. "Too floppy?" She dangles a wormlike coil at him.

"No substance," he says, correcting her.

Kimmie looks offended. "What's that supposed to mean?"

But he ignores her (and the worm), instead looking down at my coil pot. "You didn't stick around at the studio on Friday."

It takes me a moment, but then I remember how he'd offered to chat. "Too much homework, I guess."

"Right." He nods.

I look down at my work, suddenly conscious of my every move.

"Another bowl?" He gestures at my piece.

"A pot," I say, as if there were some significant difference.

"Don't you ever get tired of sculpting bowl-like things?"

I shrug, feeling my face flash hot.

"So, what was your inspiration?" he continues.

I wipe my hands and pull out my drawing pad, where I've sketched it all out. "It's a spiral staircase," I say, referring to the crude pencil drawing. "I was hoping I could replicate it in a pot."

"Do you always put so much time into your plans?"

I nod, trying to get my handle just so. It keeps drooping from the weight of the twist. "I like knowing where I'm going before I even begin. It's sort of like having a map."

"Maybe that's your problem."

Problem? My face falls, just as saggily as my pot handle.

"You plan too much," he continues. "You don't let the work guide you. Maybe the piece doesn't want to be a staircase. Maybe it wants to be a slide."

"In other words, my pot doesn't work?"

"It doesn't have a pulse," he says.

"*I* have a pulse." Kimmie offers him her wrist. "Wanna check?"

Spencer shakes his head, suggesting to Kimmie that she worry less about her pulse and more about her lack of focus.

"Can you believe that ass?" she says, once he's out of earshot. She murders her clay worm with a wooden spatula.

I shake my head and chew my bottom lip, my face grew hot from the sting of his words.

"Oh, puh-leeze," she says, obviously noticing my funk. "I wouldn't put much stock into what he said. He's obviously just being pissy because you didn't play in his sandbox after school."

"Excuse me?"

"Because you didn't stick around to chat with him in the studio the other day." She rolls her eyes, frustrated at having to explain this to me.

I shrug, watching as my handle falls off completely.

"Maybe he's the one who left that gift," she continues. "I mean, he obviously wants to see you in your pj's."

"And tell me, oh, wise one, why is that obvious?"

"Hmmm. . . . I wonder," she says, nodding toward the front of the room, where Spencer is sitting at Ms. Mazur's desk, staring right at us.

26

I'M JUST ABOUT TO JOIN KIMMIE AND WES in the cafeteria for lunch when Matt crosses my path from out of nowhere, not even two steps past the soda machines.

"A ninety-eight," he beams.

"Huh?" I ask, feeling my face twist up.

"On the French quiz," he explains, giving his back a good pat. "It would have been a hundred, but I screwed up with the *le-la*-masculine-feminine thing."

"That's great," I say, "about the ninety-eight, I mean."

"So, where have you been? I've been trying to call you. I wanted to give you the good news."

"Right," I say, suddenly remembering how my mom mentioned that he'd been trying to reach me. "Things have been sort of intense lately."

"Anything you want to talk about?"

I shake my head and peer over his shoulder, noticing

Kimmie and Wes already sitting in our designated spots.

I wave, and Kimmie gives me a thumbs-up, but Wes, obviously still miffed about our last conversation, barely even nods in what would have to be the saddest attempt at a nonverbal greeting ever.

"So, I hate to ask you this," Matt continues, "but, any chance you can help me again for the next quiz? I mean, I know it's a hassle, so if you want, I can pay you."

"No," I say. "It's fine."

"Are you sure?"

He continues to jabber on—something about not wanting to let his grades slip and some scholarship he's applying for. I'm only half listening.

Because Ben just walked in.

He takes a seat in the corner, but he isn't eating. Instead, he opens a book and starts to write something, but I can tell he's faking it, because he's staring right at me now.

"You still fixated on that guy?" Matt asks, following my glance.

I shake my head, reluctant to tell him about our date, especially since I doubt we'll be going on anymore. "I guess I didn't realize he had this lunch period," I say, practically stuttering.

"Probably because he spends most of his lunch periods in the library—at least, that's what I heard. I also heard that parents have been calling the school like crazy to get him kicked out."

"For real?"

"It's not exactly a secret. Didn't you hear about that

freshman girl—Dorothy, or Daisy, or something like that. . . ? She said he was following her the other day. She made a big scene about it—started crying and saying her parents were going to sue. Everybody wants him gone."

"Apparently so," I say, motioning to John Kenneally and a pack of his soccer buddies. They're standing in a huddle just a few feet behind Ben.

"What do you think they're up to?" Matt asks.

I shake my head just as John approaches Ben, soup bowl in hand. He pauses right behind him to await more attention.

And it works. People start snickering. The lemmings are pointing. Mr. Muse, the gym teacher, turns his back, pretending not to see anything.

John raises the bowl high above Ben's head.

"No!" I shout, from somewhere deep inside me—I have no idea if the word actually comes out.

By the time Ben notices, it's too late. John has dumped tomato soup down the front of Ben's shirt. It drips down in a muted red patch, covering Ben's chest, as if his heart were bleeding out.

Someone yells out that Ben murdered another girlfriend. Someone else coughs out the words *killer go home*. And it's high fives all around for John Kenneally and his cohorts.

Still, Ben doesn't fight back. He merely wipes his shirt and sits there, pretending none of this bothers him.

It bothers me, though.

And so, without even thinking, I grab a stack of napkins and head over to his table. "Can I join you?" I ask

Ben, sitting down before he can answer.

"I don't think I'll be sticking around," he says.

"You're not going to let them get to you, are you?" I motion to John and his friends, including Davis Miller, my guitar-playing neighbor, now sitting at the next table over. Davis glares at me with those giant brown eyes, wondering, maybe, why I'm sitting here.

And maybe I'm wondering the same thing.

"Why do you think I'm being as calm as I am?" Ben asks.

"Good question. Why are you being this calm?"

"Because they expect something else. But I won't give them that. I won't give them a reason to expel me. I need to be here."

"Need?"

He nods. "By the way, you're not having the soup today, are you?"

"I think you've probably had enough for everybody," I say, passing him the stack of napkins.

"You don't have to do this."

"You're covered in Campbell soup heinousness," I say. "It looks like you could use a little help."

"No. I mean, you don't have to do *this*—commit social suicide over me."

I glance over at Kimmie and Wes, a full five tables away. Kimmie tosses her hands up, silently asking me what I'm doing. But I look away.

"I'm not the one who needs saving, remember?" he continues.

"You mean, what happened in the parking lot?"

He stops wiping his shirt and leans in close. "I mean what's going to happen if you're not careful."

"Are you the one who called me Saturday night?"

He shakes his head, his eyes widening. "Is there something you want to tell me?"

"No," I say. "There's something that *you* need to tell *me*. What were you thinking by showing up at my house and telling me my life is in danger? That's not exactly normal, you know."

"I was thinking I want to help you."

"Well, you have a funny way of showing it."

"I'm not your enemy here, Camelia."

"Did you leave me that gift and the note?"

His face knots up in confusion. "What gift? What note?"

I take a deep breath, trying to be calm, but my heart is pounding, and I keep fidgeting in my seat. "Is this some weird plan of yours to try and get close to me?"

"I want to help you," he repeats.

I look around the cafeteria, noticing how the commotion has eased up a bit.

"You have something to tell me, don't you?" he asks.

"I don't know." I glance up at the clock. Only three minutes before the bell rings.

"How about we get together tonight? Will you be free around six?"

"I have to work."

"Then how about tomorrow?"

I shake my head, suddenly feeling the urge to flee.

"Just say yes," he insists.

"I can't."

"Is it because you're afraid of me?"

I bite my bottom lip, not knowing what the right answer even is. Ben tries to touch my forearm, but I pull away just in time.

"I have to go." I get up from the table.

"That isn't an answer. Come meet me tonight."

I shake my head and turn away, before he has the chance to ask me anything else.

Before I have the chance to change my answer to yes.

27

What was she thinking with that scene in the cafeteria? I know she did it for attention.

What I don't know is why she acts like this. You'd think she'd be grateful for the gift I left her. That she wouldn't go behind my back, ignoring my warning like we never even talked.

Sometimes I wish I could just get her out of my head, but she's everywhere, in my thoughts, in my dreams. She's the first thing I think about when I wake up, the last thing to haunt me before I go to sleep. If she'd just listen to me, everything could be ok.

28

I SPEND THE NEXT COUPLE OF DAYS keeping my distance from Ben. I don't linger after chemistry, even though I know he wants to talk. I don't sit with him in the cafeteria, even though that's where he's been eating lunch lately.

And I don't let him touch me.

Even though he's been trying to.

He's been trying to hand me things, and brush by me, and make it so that we bump into each other in the hallway. Kimmie has this theory that Ben must have a touching fetish. Wes thinks the touching has more to do with control—sort of like he's marking his own personal groping territory. "He knows you don't want to be touched," he explains, "and so he tries to do it anyway, to show you who's in charge."

Personally, I don't know what the answer is. I just want it all to stop.

The thing is, ever since I've avoided talking to him, my life *has* somewhat gone back to normal, as evidenced by this afternoon.

It's after school and Kimmie, Wes, and I are at Brain Freeze sharing a Banana Bucket—basically a huge banana split with three shovels for spoons.

"People are still talking about the little scene you caused in the cafeteria the other day," Wes says.

"I didn't cause it. John did, remember?" I thwack his shovel from my side of the pail, silently marking my ice-cream territory.

"Touchy, touchy," he says.

"No pun intended, of course," Kimmie adds. "So, where were you last night?" She looks at Wes. "I tried to call you, but your dad wouldn't say where you were."

"Nothing big." He shrugs, his mouth full of ice cream. "Just out stalking some girls, taking random pictures of them when they least suspect it and leaving gifts outside their bedroom windows. The work of a stalker is never done, I tell you." He lets out an exhausted sigh and then gives me a pointed look.

"I said I was sorry," I remind him.

"I prefer a lot more groveling with my apologies. But, since we're on the topic of stalkers, did you guys hear about that Debbie girl? I heard Ben's been following her, leaving notes on her locker, totally screwing with her head."

"Wait, is this girl a freshman?" I ask, remembering how Matt mentioned something similar.

Wes nods. "Debbie Marcus, captain of the JV swim team, currently dating Todd McCaffrey—"

"And supposedly getting stalked by Butcher Boy?" Kimmie interrupts.

"You heard it here first."

"Exactly," Kimmie snaps, dropping her shovel to the table. "How come *I* didn't hear this first?"

"Getting a little behind on the gossip train, are we?" Wes smirks.

"No," Kimmie says. "I just don't hang out with freshmen."

"For your information, I heard this from a fellow junior, who shall remain nameless."

"Whatever." Kimmie rolls her eyes. "Did your mysterious informant give you any details?"

Wes shrugs, but he clearly has nothing else to add.

"The juice is in the details, my boy," she says. "Better take a seat in the caboose and let *me* drive this train. I'll get the scoop."

"Well, get this scoop," Wes says. "I did spot the freshman in question chewing Ben out today and throwing a crumpled wad of paper in his face."

"A crumpled wad of paper, or one of the suspicious locker notes of which you speak?"

Wes's face crinkles up. "How the hell am I supposed to know?"

"I repeat," Kimmie says. "Let *me* drive this train."

I take a giant shovelful of ice cream and lean back in my seat.

"Have you told your parents about all your drama?" Kimmie asks, turning to me.

"Not yet."

"If it's really creeping you out, I think you should tell them," she says. "I bet some loser at school has seen you hanging out with Ben and thinks it'd be funny to mess with you."

"Maybe," I say. "That's why I just want to wait a little longer—see if I can figure this out on my own first, instead of turning it into a big deal."

"A victim's last words." Wes snickers.

"Speaking of . . . " Kimmie says, perhaps sensing my desire to change the subject, "my mom's become my dad's victim. You should have seen the way he was ogling Nate's babysitter last night. Granted, the girl was wearing a hoochie-mama mini with a belly shirt and streetwalker boots, but still, she's barely even eighteen years old."

"Care to lend me her number?" Wes asks.

"Get in line behind my horn-toad dad. After Hoochie-Mama left, he kept trying to convince my mom to shorten her skirt a full ten inches."

"Now there's a sobering image," he says.

"Not as sobering as you with a streaky orange face," she tells him. "I told you . . . self-tanners need to be applied evenly."

"At least it's faded a bit," I say, coming to his defense.

"My dad wouldn't even look at me," he says. "He said the sight of me made him sick."

"So, does the sight of himself make him want to

croak?" Kimmie asks. "I mean, let's face it, he's not exactly Calvin Klein material."

"Or even Target menswear material." I grimace.

"Doesn't matter." Wes shakes his head. "Nothing matters to him unless I bring home some eye candy."

"Say no more." Kimmie sighs. "What time shall I be there?"

"Thanks, anyway." Wes smiles. "But he'd never buy it. He knows you too well."

"Well, then, how about Camelia?"

"Hold up," Wes says, gesturing toward the door with his shovel. "Butcher Boy at two o'clock."

I turn to look, and notice Ben standing by the doorway. "What do you think he wants?" I ask, sinking down into my seat.

"Well, this *is* an ice-cream shop," Kimmie says. "Give the boy the benefit of the butterscotch sundae."

"No deal." Wes winks at me. "He's spotted you. He's coming this way. He totally wants to feel you up."

I glance back in the direction of the door, but Ben is already standing at our table.

"Hey, there." He nods at Kimmie and Wes, but then focuses on me. "Do you have a second?"

"I'm actually kind of busy right now."

He looks at the bucket of ice cream, almost empty now. "Please. It'll only take a second."

"Can't you tell me now?"

"We're all ears," Wes says, sitting up straight in his seat.

"I was actually hoping we could talk in private."

"What difference does it make?" Kimmie says. "We're her best friends. She's going to tell us just as soon as you leave, anyway."

I kick Kimmie under the table, thinking about the note again.

"It's okay," I say, finally. "But I only have a minute."

"Thirty seconds until I polish off the rest of this bucket," Wes says, scraping his shovel along the bottom of the pail.

Ben leads me to a booth in the corner, and we sit down opposite one another.

"How come you've been avoiding me?" he asks.

I take a deep breath, wondering where I should begin, noticing the urgency in his voice. His face is flushed, and he's leaning in close.

"Because it isn't practical," he continues. "We need to work together. How else are we going to do our labs?"

"This is about chemistry?"

"No." He sighs. "It isn't."

"Is it more about how something horrible is supposed to happen to me?"

"This isn't fun for me," he insists. "And this isn't some excuse to try and get close to you."

"Then what?"

"You *know* what. So, maybe the questions we need to ask ourselves are *who* and *why*."

"Wait," I say. "I'm a little confused." I glance over at Kimmie and Wes. Kimmie licks down the length of her shovel, trying to get me to laugh.

"I make you nervous, don't I?" His eyes draw an invisible line down the center of my face, lingering on my neck as I swallow.

"Just tell me," I say. "What do you want?"

"To help you," he reminds me.

"Help me with what? I don't need any help."

"Look," he begins, "I know this sounds crazy, but if you don't let me help you, something really bad is going to happen."

"Like what?"

"Not here," he says, looking over his shoulder to make sure no one's listening in. Let's go someplace and talk about it."

"I'm not going anywhere."

"Please," he insists.

I glance back at Kimmie and Wes. Wes, clearly aware that I'm upset, looks ready to pounce. Kimmie's practically sitting in his lap trying to hold him back.

"What do you say?" Ben continues. "Will you come with me now?"

"And then you'll leave me alone?"

"I can't promise you that. But I can try and make things more clear."

I shake my head, telling myself this isn't a good idea.

But I decide to go with him anyway.

29

I TELL KIMMIE AND WES TO WAIT for me at Brain Freeze while I give Ben exactly fifteen minutes to state his case.

They're not crazy about my going, but since the beach is only at the end of the street, and since I make them promise to come and look for me if I'm not back in twenty minutes flat, they finally agree.

And I go—part of me relieved to get this over with, another part scared to death of what Ben has to say.

We walk in silence down the main drag, until the ocean begins to come into view. Just as I expected, there are plenty of people sprinkled about—a throng of fisher-men casting their lines out on the pier, a few dog-walkers along the shore, and a handful of kids playing on the swings.

Ben leads us to a spot up on the rocks, where we can look out at the ocean and still hear the rush of cars speeding by on the road behind us. We sit down facing one another, but Ben keeps looking out at the water, as if seeing me now is even harder for him to deal with than whatever he has to say.

"So, we're here," I venture, giving a nervous tug to my ponytail.

Ben nods and looks at me finally, his expression changed—less frantic, a mixture of resolution and sullenness, maybe.

"What is it?" I ask, noticing how his eyes are liquid gray.

"It happened at a place like this," he says.

"What did?"

He palms a polished rock and squeezes it hard, as though it gives him the courage to speak. "I know you've heard stuff about me."

"Are you talking about your girlfriend?"

"Julie," he whispers, his voice all scratchy, as if speaking her name were like glass in his throat. "I know what people say. But I didn't kill her. What happened was an accident. It's important to me that you know that." His eyes bear down on mine, as he checks to see if I do believe him. But I avoid his gaze.

"We were hiking up on a cliff that day," he continues. "There was a beach below and lots of rocks. We had just gotten into an argument."

I nod, remembering how Matt said he'd heard Ben had a temper.

"I grabbed her arm," he says. "But she pulled away,

toward the edge of the cliff. I tried to lunge at her, to stop her from moving back, but it was too late." He looks back out over the water, his voice barely above a whisper now. "She fell."

I glance at his forearm, where his long-sleeved T-shirt covers the scar, wondering where the gash came from—if maybe the argument got physical and Julie put up a fight. Or if maybe he climbed down after her and tried to save her life.

"Why were you grabbing on to her?" I ask. "Why was she backing away from you?"

"Because I'm different than most people."

"Excuse me?"

He puts on his sunglasses, so I can't see how upset he is—how his eyes have reddened and the skin around them has gotten blotchy. "Remember that day in the parking lot, when I pushed you out of the way of that car?"

I nod.

"I touched you that day—on your stomach. And I got this weird sensation—like something bad was going to happen. It was the same thing in chemistry—when I touched your hand—only the feeling was stronger."

"Wait," I say, my face bunching up in confusion. "What are you talking about?"

"I sense things," he explains, "when I touch people. Sometimes I see things, too. It's why I took off in the parking lot after I knew you were okay. I didn't want to deal with what I was sensing. I wanted to pretend like it never even happened—like I never even saw you."

"Are you trying to tell me you're some kind of psychic?"

"Just think about it," he says, ignoring the question. "Why do you think I've been touching you so much lately? I had to be sure."

"Sure about what?"

"That your life is at stake," he reminds me.

I take a deep breath, my mind spinning with questions.

"I felt something that day with Julie, too," he continues. "Not danger, though. I sensed she was lying. When I touched her, I could picture how she was seeing somebody else, how she had cheated on me that very same day. I asked her about it, too, and she confessed to the whole thing. Only, I wouldn't let it go there. I had to know with whom and for how long. And so I gripped her harder, the picture becoming clearer. I could see my best friend. I could picture the two of them together—lying in the sand, kissing by the shore . . ." He takes a deep breath and lets it filter out slowly. "No matter what anybody says, I never meant to hurt her. The thing is, I gripped too hard. And that scared her."

"Which is why she backed away," I say, putting the pieces together.

"It's called psychometry," he explains. "The ability to sense things through touch. People who have it practice it differently—for some, it's about placing an object up to their foreheads and getting a picture; for others it's about hearing sounds or smelling scents when they touch something. For me, there's a fine line between touching someone and hurting them—and I can't let myself cross it." He swallows hard and looks down at his hands.

"Once I reach that point, and get too close," he continues, "something inside me switches gears, and I lose control. I even lose the ability to reason. It's like my body's there, but my mind isn't."

"So, what do you do?" I ask.

"I try to counter it with stuff, like with meditation and tae kwon do—stuff that helps keep me in the moment—but it's still hard. And still scary. It's why I stay away from everybody. It's why I was so standoffish with you. After what happened with Julie, I didn't want to know anyone else's fate or picture anyone else's secrets."

"And so you expected to live a life completely free of touching people."

"It was working for me up until a few months ago."

"When you touched me."

He nods and clenches his teeth. The angles of his face grow sharp. "At first I wanted to ignore what I felt, but my conscience wouldn't let me. I mean, what if something bad happened to you because I did nothing to stop it?"

"I guess that explains a lot," I say, thinking how he's always late to class—to avoid careening into people in the hallways—and how that first time, when I approached him at his locker, he didn't want to admit to ever having seen me before. "So, what does all this mean for me?" I ask. "You touch me and sense stuff?"

He nods and slides his sunglasses back on top of his

head to reveal his eyes, all puffy and raw. "That's how I know you're in danger."

"And so, what's supposed to happen?"

He stares at me for several moments, not saying anything, as though memorizing the contours of my face.

"Just tell me," I insist, sensing his hesitation.

"I can see your body," he whispers, finally.

"My body? As in my *dead* body?"

He nods, and my stomach lurches, like I'm going to be sick.

"At first I wasn't sure," he says. "It was just a feeling. But, then, on our picnic date, when you kissed me . . . that's when I knew."

I take a deep breath, unable to ask him anything more.

"Are you okay?"

I shake my head, suddenly needing some air, even though we're outside. I glance down at my watch, suspecting it's been way more than fifteen minutes.

"Please don't tell anyone about any of this," he says. "It's private."

"My being in danger is private?"

"Well, no, not that, but this touch thing with me is. And I'd kind of like to keep it that way—at least for now."

"As in *our little secret*?"

"I guess it is." He nods, and I study his face, searching for some knowing glare or pointed look—something to indicate that he's the one who left that gift—but I just can't tell.

"Can we maybe talk later?" he asks. "Can I call you?"

"I need to go," I say, tripping over the words.

He mutters something about promising to help me—about being determined to get to the bottom of this—but I'm not really listening.

I get up from the rock, suddenly feeling like I'm being watched. I turn to look over my shoulder and spot Kimmie and Wes, sitting over by the swings, watching me from afar.

30

She just won't listen. And so I've started
a plan. I just hope she appreciates all my
efforts—all my work to make her happy.
Once and for all.

31

*A*FTER MY TALK WITH BEN, Wes and Kimmie are all twenty-questions-times-a-hundred about what he had to say.

But I just don't feel like talking about it.

Instead, I stare out the window as Wes drives us home, watching the swirl of colors, of houses mixed with buildings and trees, all blending together into one big blur.

"Come on," Kimmie begs. "If you're not going to give us the full story, then how about just the CliffsNotes version?"

I shake my head, still unnerved by my conversation with Ben, by the image of his girlfriend as she fell over the cliff that day, and the look of horror that must have covered her face when she saw him lunge for her.

"Paging Camelia Chameleon," Wes says, cupping his mouth and speaking through his makeshift megaphone.

"Maybe she needs some water splashed on her face," Kimmie suggests.

"All I've got is a day-old Big Gulp," he says, jiggling a supersize soda cup. He peers at me in his rearview mirror, but I look back toward the street, suddenly very anxious to get home.

"Do you want me to come in with you?" Kimmie asks, once we pull up in front of my house.

"No, thanks," I say, managing a smile. "I'll call you, okay?"

She nods, and I go up the front steps and straight inside to the kitchen, part of me relieved to find a note from my mom saying that one of the teachers at the yoga studio called in sick and she's covering for her, and another part scared to death to be alone.

In my room, I pull down my shades and make sure both windows are closed and locked, unable to shake Ben's words.

It's barely even five o'clock. I have at least another hour until my dad gets home. And so I camp out at my computer desk and google the term *psychometry*, half hoping it's just some made-up word, that Ben doesn't know what he's talking about.

But it pops up right away.

Psychometry: the ability to "see" through touch: to learn about an object's history or read into a person's future by touching it or him.

I sit down on the corner of my bed and snuggle against my stuffed polar bear, trying to figure out what all of this means—what it'll mean if I choose to believe him. I stare back at my reflection in the dresser mirror—hair pulled back, heart-shaped face, eyes set wide apart—wondering what Ben really sees when he touches me.

And what I would look like dead.

A moment later the phone rings, startling me. I stare at it, debating whether or not to pick it up—if whoever left me that gift knows I'm alone.

Four rings. Five.

I finally pick it up, but it's a dial tone before I can even speak. I take a deep breath, trying to exhale away the knot in my chest, wishing I had taken Kimmie up on her offer to come in.

Instead of clicking the phone back off, I leave it on and head downstairs to the basement, where I've got a pottery studio set up in the corner, complete with table, sculpting tools, and potter's wheel. I take the tie off a bag of clay, cut myself a nice, thick slice, and then thwack it down against my board. The clay is smooth and moist beneath my fingertips. I roll it out between my palms, resisting the urge to think too much or plan anything out, and instead I take notice of the texture of the clay and how it shapes in my hands.

"What does this sculpture want to be?" I ask, taking Spencer's words to heart about letting the work guide me for a change.

I continue to punch, prod, and pull at my clay for at least another hour, but somehow all I have to show for it in the end is a long, stringy piece with handles at both ends, like a jump rope. Pretty much as pulseless as you can get.

I'm just about to roll it up into a ball and begin again

when I hear something—a banging noise coming from upstairs.

"Dad?" I call.

But he doesn't answer.

I resume my work, chalking the noise up to a door slamming outside or a truck driving by. But then I hear it again. Only it's louder this time.

Slowly, I approach the stairwell, catching a glimpse of how dark it is outside through the windows of our basement. I glance at my watch. It's already nearing eight o'clock.

So, where is my dad? And why isn't Mom home yet?

The banging sound continues as I make my way upstairs and click on the kitchen light. But then the noise stops completely.

"Dad?" I call again, wondering if maybe he forgot his house key. I move into the living room to look out the front window, but the driveway's still empty. No one's home yet.

My pulse races as I approach the door. I look out the peephole, but there's no one standing out there. I tell myself it must have been a door-to-door salesperson and that he or she must have moved on already.

A moment later, I hear a pelting noise coming from down the hall.

I take a deep breath, wishing we had an alarm system, then grab the phone to dial my dad's cell—but it won't click on, and I can't get a dial tone. Meanwhile, my cell phone's in my bedroom.

The pelting sound continues. It's followed by a loud crashing sound, like glass shattering.

Like someone's trying to break in.

My hands shaking, I snag an umbrella from the holder by the door and grip it in my hand, the tip pointed, ready for a fight. I start down the hallway, debating whether I should go to a neighbor's house instead, but I'm too afraid to go outside.

A second later, I hear a noise at the front door. I move back in that direction, noticing how the doorknob is jiggling. The screen door opens, and the doorbell rings.

My heart hammers hard inside my chest. I peer through the peephole, almost collapsing in relief when I see who's out there.

I unlock the door and whisk it open. Kimmie's standing there, a plateful of brownies in her hands.

"What do you think you're doing?" I blurt out, pulling her inside.

"No, the question is what are *you* doing? I called your cell phone—no answer. I called your home phone—the line is busy."

"I left it off the hook," I say, remembering.

"Exactly," she huffs, thrusting the plate of brownies at me. "That's what the operator said, too."

"You called the operator?"

"Well, yeah. The whole thing smelled like fish, after all. I mean, I know you guys have call-waiting."

"Fishy or not, you scared me to bits." I look toward the hallway. The pelting sound has stopped.

"I broke your window, by the way," she says, prying the umbrella from my grip. "When you wouldn't answer the door, I thought that maybe you were taking one of your marathon baths, and so I decided to throw rocks at the bathroom window. But apparently, I got a little too aggressive, because the glass broke. Brownie?" She lifts off the plastic wrap and helps herself to one. "I hope you don't mind if a couple got smooshy. They were crammed in the basket of my bike."

"You rode here on your bike?"

"Hauled ass is more like it," she says. "Do you know how many potholes this cheapskate town has?"

"Why didn't your mom drop you off?"

"Mom's too busy trying to appease my dad, by shopping for miniskirts and thigh-high boots."

"Okay, so wait." I shake my head, my mind whirling with questions. "Why didn't you just ring the doorbell?"

"Um, yeah, hello! I rang it for, like, ten minutes straight."

"I was in the basement."

"Which is probably why you didn't hear it, Nancy Drew."

I smile, grateful for her persistence. "Well, at least you got to take out some of your aggression on the window . . . not to mention the door."

"The door?" she says, her mouth full of brownie.

"Yeah, you practically beat the door down."

"Um, no I didn't."

"You didn't pound on the door?"

"I may have rapped a couple times, but not hard. I could hear the doorbell ringing from the outside, so I knew it was working."

"Wait," I say, feeling my heart speed up again. "You didn't bang at the door? You didn't knock real hard?"

Kimmie shakes her head, a worried expression on her face.

I grab the umbrella again and step into the doorway, checking outside to see if anything looks off. But aside from Kimmie's bike, parked smack in the center of my mother's jasmine bush, everything appears fine.

"What are you thinking?" she asks.

"Someone was pounding."

"But I was outside, remember? I would have seen someone knocking."

"Not if you were out back, throwing rocks at the bathroom." I let out a giant breath and start to close the door. But that's when I see it; a shiver runs down my back.

"What's wrong?" Kimmie asks, following my glance.

I gesture toward the mailbox. The red flag is pointing up, indicating that something's in there, even though I know for a fact I checked the box on the way in and it was empty, with the flag pointing down.

"Do you want me to check?" she asks.

I shake my head, not knowing what to do—scared to know what's in there, but maybe even more scared to just leave it alone.

"What the hell did Ben say to you today?" she asks.

I continue to look outside, straining my eyes, wondering if I'm being watched at this very moment—if someone's out there lurking behind a car or down the street.

Kimmie steps outside and opens the mailbox.

"What is it?" I ask.

She looks up at me, her lips parted in shock, like she doesn't want to say.

"Tell me," I demand.

She reluctantly takes it out and turns it over so I can see.

It's another eight-by-ten photograph of me. Only, instead of a bubbly heart surrounding my image, someone's scribbled over my face and then written the words *I'M CLOSER THAN YOU THINK* across my body in bright red marker.

I grab Kimmie, slam the door closed, and lock both locks. "Someone's watching me," I whisper.

"It's going to be okay," she says, wrapping her arms around me.

I wait for her to explain it all away—to tell me this is another joke, or blame the whole thing on Wes. But instead she remains silent.

32

*K*IMMIE BRINGS ME A CUP OF my mom's dandelion tea and then sits down beside me on the living room sofa. "It was the strongest thing I could find."

"My mom likes to keep a chemical-free home, remember?"

"Right." She fishes inside her satin-lined clutch for a pad of paper and a pen. "So, I really think we need to tell your parents."

I nod, glancing down at the coffee table, where my mom's old family album is still opened up to the picture of her and Aunt Alexia. They're twelve and seven, respectively, and they're posing in front of the Christmas tree, candy canes in their hands.

There's a bright smile on Aunt Alexia's face, and so I know my grandmother wasn't the one taking the picture. Aunt Alexia looks way too happy, after all.

I close the album, remembering the last time Aunt Alexia was in a mental hospital and how my mom ended up in a hole of depression for over two weeks—two weeks of barely getting out of bed and having to be reminded to eat, sleep, and bathe.

"I don't want to bother my parents with this just yet," I say finally.

"And you don't think an untimely death will be a bother?"

"Just give me a couple more days," I insist. "I want to try and figure things out on my own."

"Well, you're *not* alone." She slips on her cat-eye glasses and stares at me from above the rims. "So, let's review. What do we know for sure?"

"I'm being followed."

"Right," she says, jotting it down.

"Someone's watching me, and he's getting closer."

"Do you have any idea who this someone might be?"

"Well, I'm assuming it's a guy."

"Rule number one," she says, crossing her legs at her faux-tattoo-adorned ankle, where a smiling Betty Boop winks up in my direction. "Never assume."

"But it was a male voice who called me, remember?"

"Male, schmale. Just look at Wes. He can change his voice on cue—and not just guy voices, either. He's an equal-opportunity impersonator."

"You still think this is Wes?"

"All I'm saying is that we can't rule anyone out. Also, haven't you ever heard of voice-changers? They can make any female sound male and vice versa."

"But he told me I was pretty."

"You *are* pretty, so what's your point?"

I shrug and glance toward the picture window, tempted to pull down the blind.

"We also shouldn't rule out the whole conspiracy theory," she continues.

"You think this could be more than one person?"

"Rule number two: anything's possible. Which brings me to my next question: what did Ben say to you today?"

"That he can see me dead."

"That's normal."

"I can explain."

"Okay, so rule number three," she says, already annoyed. "Stop making excuses for Ben."

"I'm not making excuses," I say. "He's psychometric."

"I know. A total nut job, right?"

"Not psychotic, *psychometric*: he can sense things through touch."

"Excuse me?"

I take a deep breath and explain the whole thing— everything he told me and all that I learned online.

"So, let me get this straight," she says, taking a sip of my tea. "The boy touches stuff and can sense the future?"

"Sometimes the future, sometimes the past. Sometimes he sees an image. Other times it's just a feeling."

"Like a crystal ball," she says.

"Minus the ball."

"Okay, so, balls aside, how can I get him to touch

me? I need to know if John Kenneally is going to ask me out."

"He doesn't like to touch anyone," I say, to clarify matters.

"Except you," she smirks.

"Except me," I whisper, swallowing hard.

"Oh my god, do you know how hot that is?" She fans herself with her pad of paper. "I mean, even if it is complete and total BS."

"You don't believe him?"

"Oh, puh-leeze," she says, still fanning. "He's obviously just looking for excuses to feel you up. You got to give the boy credit for creativity, though. I mean, that's some pretty original BS."

I shake my head, disappointed that she doesn't believe him, but not sure I can blame her.

"When are you supposed to see him again?" she asks.

"He said he wanted to talk later."

"Later as in tonight?"

I nod, wondering if it was him beating at the door. "Just don't say anything, okay? About his psychometric powers, I mean. He doesn't want anyone to know."

"Honey, you have bigger things to worry about than keeping secrets." She looks at the eight-by-ten photo again. "It was taken at the park on the day of your date."

I nod, noticing the grassy hill in the background behind me. "But it was taken after the date," I say, pointing out my positioning—how I'm walking away from the hill, back toward the car.

"So, Ben was still behind you," she says.

"No," I say, correcting her. "Ben was hightailing it out of there, remember?"

"Maybe that's just what he wanted you to think. Maybe he started to take off, but then when he saw you do the same, he snapped a picture behind your back—*literally*."

"I also bumped into John Kenneally at the park," I say, suddenly remembering it.

"And I'm just hearing about this *now*?"

"His team practices there every Saturday afternoon, by the way."

"But it can't be him," she says, running her finger over the pen scribbles on the photo. You can see where the marks are etched into the paper, like whoever did this was really angry. "This isn't John's style."

"How do *you* know?"

"I just do, okay? End of story."

"Which brings us to rule number one," I say. "Never make assumptions, remember?"

"No," she corrects. "It actually brings us to rule number four: don't trust anyone."

"Not even you?"

"Okay, except me and your parents. And rule number five: don't go out anywhere alone. Call me. I'll come."

"Even tonight?"

She lowers her cat-eye glasses to the tip of her nose. "What's tonight?"

"I want to talk to Ben some more."

"Okay, are you seriously as psychotic as he is?"

"Not psychotic, *psychometric*."

"Whatever," she snaps. "It's a bad idea."

"Well, it's the only one I've got right now. I mean, just think about it. Weird stuff is happening to me. Ben claims to sense I'm in danger. Even if he *is* lying, maybe I'll be able to figure that out just by talking to him."

"And, if he's not . . . and you are in danger?"

"Then I'll be able to hear him out," I say, surprised she's even entertaining the idea that he's telling the truth. "I think I owe myself that, don't you?"

"I think you should put his touchable powers to the test," she says, gesturing toward the photo. "Have him touch some of this stuff and see what he has to say about it. My guess is you'll be able to smell the BS from a mile away."

A moment later, there's a knock on the door, making me jump. My knee bumps the teacup, and the liquid goes spilling across the cherrywood table in a long, narrow stream that reminds me of blood.

I return the photo to the envelope and then stuff it inside my sweatshirt. Meanwhile, Kimmie grabs my wheel-spun bowl from the end table.

The screen door swings open, and the knob jiggles back and forth. Someone's trying to get in.

Kimmie approaches the door, the bowl positioned high above her head.

A second later, I hear it—a key pushing into the lock. The door swings open.

"Hey, there, lovey," my mom says, tossing her yoga mat to the floor.

My dad follows close behind her, squawking that the line's been busy for the past two hours.

"Sorry," I say. "I thought I hung it up. Where have you guys been?"

"Dinner," Mom says, planting a kiss on my cheek. She eyes the pottery bowl, still in fighting position high above Kimmie's head. "Is everything okay in here?"

"You bet," Kimmie says, returning the bowl to the table. "I mean, aside from thinking you might have been a crazy ax murderer trying to break in."

"But all's well now," I say, wishing I had a muzzle for her.

Mom gives Kimmie a smooch on the cheek as well. "Are you girls hungry? I have some leftover lettuce cups in the fridge."

"Run for your lives," Dad jokes.

"Actually, I should probably get going," Kimmie says. "I have some design stuff I want to finish. I'm trying to get into a workshop at the Fashion Institute. You have to submit a portfolio even to be considered."

"That's great," my mother chirps, catching a glimpse of her own yogified apparel in the hallway mirror.

"Wait, what about studying tonight?" I ask, giving Kimmie a pointed look.

Kimmie's face scrunches up for about half a second before she finally gets the picture. "If you absolutely have to."

"I do."

"It's almost nine o'clock," Dad says. "How much later do you expect to work?"

"How about I call you in a little bit?" Kimmie suggests. "I really think we should go over that list of rules one more time."

I nod as my dad lets her out. A giant pit forms in the center of my gut, because I know that there's no convincing Kimmie—not tonight, anyway. If I want to talk to Ben, I'm totally on my own.

33

I HEAD DOWN THE HALLWAY to my room, suddenly realizing that Kimmie left me with the honor of telling my parents about the broken bathroom window. So while they cuddle up on the living room sofa, I go check out the damage.

It's even worse than I thought. Not just a tiny crack or hole; the window is completely smashed in.

I grab a dustpan and brush, and start to sweep it all up, but then I notice a trace of mud on the floor. It trails across the ceramic tiles to the hallway and then toward my bedroom.

My mind races. I glance back at the window. Both the pane and screen have been pulled up. Like someone climbed through.

I look toward the shower, wondering if someone might be in there now. Slowly I approach it, my pulse quickening. I snatch a razor from the vanity, preparing myself to fight. In one quick motion, I whisk the curtain open and let out a gasp.

But luckily it's empty.

My chest heaving, I try to get a grip, remind myself that my parents are only four rooms away.

I inch down the hallway to my room. The door is closed, even though I know I left it open. The razor still gripped between my fingers, I turn the knob, step inside, and see it: the word *BITCH* written across my dresser mirror in dark red lipstick.

34

MY HAND TREMBLES over my mouth. I approach the dresser. There's a mysterious pile of fabric sitting on top of it. I let out a breath and move a little closer, almost startled by my own reflection in the mirror, by the way the word *BITCH* cuts across my face and makes me look like I'm bleeding.

I look down at the fabric—the pale pink color, the soft fleece fabric, and the bits of ribbon. It's the pajamas he bought me. They've been torn into a million tiny shreds, as if with a knife.

I glance over at the corner of the room, where I've been keeping the gift box and packaging. It's all been ripped open. The note and tissue paper have been tossed onto the floor.

Still shaking, I drop the razor and close my eyes, cover my ears. I feel myself breathe in and out, trying to calm myself down, even though every inch of me wants to scream.

I take several steps backward, preparing to exit the room, peering out of the corner of my eye at my closet door, which is still closed. Instead of checking inside it, I hurry down the hallway and into the living room. My parents are sitting on the sofa. Tears stain my mother's face.

"Mom?"

"Cam, can you just give us a few minutes?" Dad asks, his back to me.

My mom sobs—like I've never heard her before.

"What happened?" I ask, taking another step, noticing my mom's cell phone gripped in her hands.

Dad turns to me finally. "Your mom just got some unsettling news."

"About Aunt Alexia," Mom says, trying to regain her composure.

"What about her?" I ask.

"She's back in the hospital," she says, tearing up even more; it's as if saying it aloud only makes it worse.

I linger a moment, watching her sob, waiting for one of them to fill me in on what's going on, but neither of them answers me. It's like I'm no longer there. I turn away finally and head back to my room.

The closet is in full view.

My heart racing, I grab an old trophy from my desk, clutch it above my head, and pull the door open.

But there's no one in there, and nothing looks awry.

I let out a breath and try calling Kimmie, but her mom tells me she went to the library. I dial her cell phone, but it goes straight to voice mail. Wes isn't home, either.

Not knowing where to turn or what to do, I wash the word *BITCH* from the mirror, as if it were never even there. Then I sweep the pajama remains into the lingerie box and stuff it under my bed, completely out of sight.

My mom's still crying in the living room; I try calling Kimmie's cell again. No luck. Finally, I hear the cabinet door slam shut in the kitchen. I head out there, only to find Dad pouring gin into one of Mom's favorite glasses— even though she never drinks. Even though I didn't even know they kept a secret stash.

"Dad?" I ask, catching him by surprise.

He turns to face me. "Your mom's really upset," he says, trying to explain the gin away.

"I know, but I really need to talk to you about something."

"Can it wait until morning?"

I suck in my lips, noticing how my dad's eyes have reddened, like he's just as upset as Mom.

"The window in the bathroom is broken," I say, finally, testing the waters. "It was an accident. Kimmie threw a rock and it—"

"That's fine," he says, cutting me off. "I'll take care of it later." And with that, he goes back into the living room, where Mom is curled up.

Back in my room, I try calling Kimmie yet again. Still no luck. And so I sit down on the edge of my bed, trying to hold it all together, even though I feel like I'm coming apart.

I grab Ben's phone number from my jewelry box, scared to death to call him, but I really need to talk to somebody. And maybe he's all I have right now.

I start to dial his number, but then I hear something outside my window—the sound of an engine revving.

I move to the window to look. Ben cuts his engine, hops off the motorcycle, and makes his way to the front door. But before he gets there, I call out his name, surprising even myself.

He waves when he sees me. The moon casts its light over him—over the sharp angles of his face and his dark gray eyes.

Without saying a word, I stuff the photos into a bag along with the note and the shredded fabric, pull up the screen, and climb outside.

35

*B*EN SUGGESTS THAT WE SIT ON my front steps, but after everything that's happened tonight, I really just want to get away.

"Are you sure?" he asks.

I nod, and he studies me for just a second, as though trying to decide. But then he hands me his helmet and tells me to hold on tight.

I wrap my arms around his waist, and we take off down the road. The buzz of his motor awakens my senses, makes me feel more in the moment than ever. I must have driven down this street a million times, but I never noticed the explosion of color—how the neon lights from store signs and buildings illuminate the pavement in bright strips of red, gold, and blue.

We reach a stoplight and Ben glances back at me. Later, he turns and gives me a slight smile. Meanwhile, I have no idea where he's taking me. I just know that the cool, salty breeze tangling the ends of my hair is beyond intoxicating.

I rest my head against his back and breathe in his sugary scent, trying to calm my nerves—to tell myself that this is okay, that we're outside, where people can see us, and that my cell phone is charged and in my bag if I need it.

Still, I've never done anything like this before. I've never just taken off out my window, not telling my parents where I was going, or acted on pure instinct, without a set plan in place.

About fifteen minutes later, Ben pulls up in front of Jet Lag, a twenty-four-hour diner famous for serving breakfast at night and dinner in the morning. He extends his hand to help me off his bike, but then pulls away, as if the mere touch of my skin were too intense.

"Sorry," he says.

I nod, full of questions, but before I can ask even one, he takes a step back and then turns to open the restaurant door for me.

The place is beyond dead—only one solitary couple in a far corner. We take the opposite corner and slide the menus out from between the salt and pepper shakers.

A waitress comes shortly after and plunks a couple of mugs down on the laminated table. "Coffee?" she asks, the pot held high.

We nod, and she fills up the mugs, muttering how we look like we could use it.

I end up ordering a plate full of cinnamon French toast even though I'm anything but hungry.

"And for you?" the waitress asks Ben.

"The same," he says, forgoing the menu completely, since it's obvious we both want to be left alone.

"You felt something just now, didn't you?" I ask, as soon as she steps away.

Ben pours sugar into his mug and stirs. "I always feel something with you."

"So, what was it? Why did you pull away?"

"First, you answer my question," he says, looking right at me. There's a trace of sweat on his brow. "What happened tonight?"

My mouth drops open in surprise. "What makes you think something happened?"

"Tell me," he insists.

I wonder how he knows, whether my eagerness to bolt gave me away, or maybe it was something else.

"Can you tell *me*?" I ask. "I mean, if you can really sense stuff the way you say you can."

"Are you testing me?"

"Maybe."

Ben reaches across the table and glides his hand over mine. He encircles my fingers and takes a full breath, sending tingles straight down my back. "Did somebody give you something?" he asks finally.

"Something . . . like what?"

"I can see broken glass," he whispers, squeezing my hand harder, "and a scribble of red—like writing. Did you get a letter or a message?"

I feel my lips tremble; I'm wondering if I should tell

him, but I'm suspicious just the same. I mean, if he were the one doing all this, he'd know exactly what happened tonight, and what the message said.

"You have to trust me," he says, as though reading my mind.

A second later, he closes his eyes and grips my hand even harder—so hard I have to pull away.

"Are you okay?" he asks, his eyes wide, like he has surprised even himself.

Before I can answer, the waitress comes to deliver our plates—thick wedges of French toast with pitchers full of syrup on the side.

"I'm sorry," he continues, referring to my hand. "Sometimes it's hard to control myself."

I nod, thinking about Julie—and how he supposedly couldn't control himself with her, either.

"What can I say to make you trust me?" he asks.

I cut a piece of my French toast, considering the question and what it would take to trust anyone right now. "Touch me again," I say, meeting his eyes, "and tell me something other than what's going on right now—something from my past, maybe. Are you able to do that?"

He nods and searches the restaurant, maybe to see if anyone is listening in. Meanwhile, I reach across the table, my palm open and waiting.

Ben takes it and closes his eyes, breathing in and out as if this takes his full concentration—as if he's trying his hardest not to hurt me again. His palm is warm against my skin. I close my eyes, too, wondering what he feels.

And if his heart is beating as fast as mine.

His fingers graze my hand, as though memorizing the lines of my palm and the skin over my bones. It's all I can do just to sit here—not to hurtle over the table and kiss him again. I open my eyes to gaze at his mouth. It quivers slightly, like he's someplace else entirely.

I'm tempted to ask what he sees, but I really don't want to break this moment.

Or have him let go.

His eyes move beneath the lids, as if he can really sense something, making me feel suddenly self-conscious. Maybe it's me who has something to hide.

"I can see you as a little girl," he whispers finally. "At least, I think it's you—same wavy blond hair, same dark green eyes. You're wearing a long yellow dress with big purple flowers, and there's tall grass all around you."

I nod, remembering the dress. A chill runs up the back of my neck.

"And you're crying," he continues. "Are you lost?"

I squeeze his hand, remembering that day in the second grade when I wandered away from the playground at school. My mother, having always kept a tight leash on me, was beyond hysterical when she got the phone call— or so everyone says—but luckily she didn't have to worry long. No sooner did the school contact her than a teacher's aide found me, crouching down and crying, worried more about my mother's reaction than about finding my way back home.

The thing is, I never intended to go very far, just over

the rocks and down the hill—just to see if I could and what it would feel like. To sneak away.

Sort of like tonight.

I pull away, not wanting to hear any more. "I believe you," I whisper, staring right at him. Ben's eyes are red, making me wonder if in some way he could feel my fear just now.

"How's the French toast?" the waitress asks, standing over our table.

"A little intense," I say.

She looks back and forth between the two of us, as though noting our expressions and the sudden flushed appearance of our faces.

"Maybe *I* should try the French toast," she says, somewhat under her breath.

A nervous giggle escapes me. Ben smiles, too. And a weird, awkward moment passes over us—as if we share a secret. As if we've known each other for years.

"It's easier to sense stuff from the past than it is to project the future," he says once the waitress leaves.

"I want to tell you about what happened tonight."

Ben nods, as though eager to hear it. And so I tell him everything, including what happened earlier in the week.

"Maybe we should call the police," he says.

"And tell them what? That you touch me and see my dead body? That I'm getting weird notes, just like that Debbie girl? I mean, do you honestly think they'll take any of it seriously?"

"I honestly think it's worth a try."

I feel my jaw stiffen, still able to picture my mom on the sofa tonight, tears soaking her face as Dad tries to console her. "My parents have enough problems to deal with right now."

"Your life *is* in danger," he reminds me. "Even the notes say that."

"So, let's figure it out." I dump the contents of my bag out on the table. "Does your power work with stuff or just people?"

"Stuff, too, but it's much harder. It isn't as intense as skin-to-skin contact—touching something with an actual pulse."

I nod, feeling my own pulse race, wondering if he notices the heat I feel on my face.

"Plus," he continues, smiling as if he *does* indeed notice, "it only works when the person has recently handled the object—when I can still feel the vibrations."

"Can you feel these vibrations?" I ask, sliding my bag, with the photos and the note, across the table.

Ben spends several moments running his fingers over and through the contents of my bag, spending the most time on the photo from tonight. He presses the edges hard, until they crinkle up.

"He's planning something," he says, finally looking up at me.

"*He?*"

"I'm pretty sure." He reaches for the note and the shreds of pajama fabric, but then shakes his head. "It's like he thinks you're ungrateful for something."

"And that's why he's leaving me stuff?"

"He's leaving you stuff because he wants you to know you're being watched."

I glance out the window. "Is he watching me right now?"

"I don't know. I'd have to touch you again."

"So, go ahead."

Ben glances at my hand but then shakes his head. "Maybe I should take a little break."

I look at the photo, all mangled and bent now. "Because you're afraid you might hurt me?"

"Because I don't want to hurt anyone ever again. It's hard to keep touching people. It takes a lot of restraint, a lot of self-control, to not squeeze too hard or push too deep. It's like my mind wants to go one way, but my body wants to go another. It's sort of like sleeping with one eye open."

"And what happens when both eyes are shut?"

Ben glares at me, unwilling to answer. And maybe he doesn't have to.

I sink back in my seat, feeling stupid for even asking. "You still blame yourself for what happened with Julie, don't you?"

"Maybe we should talk about something else."

"Is that a yes?"

"It's an 'I don't want to talk about it.'"

"Have you ever talked with anyone about it?"

He shakes his head. "Before you, I barely talked to anyone. And I definitely didn't touch them."

I bite my bottom lip, wondering what it's like to go through life without touching a single soul. "What made you stop homeschooling, then?"

"I wanted to try being normal again." He looks at his hands, his eyes still red. "But maybe normal isn't right for me."

"Will you let *me* touch *you*?"

Before he can answer, I reach my hand across the table. Ben closes his eyes, and I run my fingers over the lines in his palm. His skin is rough and callused beneath my fingertips.

"Don't," he whispers.

Still, I slide my hand back and forth over his, imagining what he senses right now—if he can feel the boiling inside me.

His eyes are still closed, and I can see the urgency in his hand. His fingers curl up, like he wants to grab me.

"Sorry." I pull away.

He opens his eyes. "You have no idea how hard this is for me."

"Which part . . . holding on or letting go?"

"Both."

I feel my lips part, suddenly conscious of my every move.

"You have no idea how hard it was for me that day in the parking lot," he continues. "It took everything I had not to touch you too hard."

I rest my hand over my stomach. "You didn't hurt me," I assure him.

"I'm glad." He smiles.

I take a bite of French toast, trying to get my mind off this aching inside my bones. Ben starts to eat, too. He chews in silence, staring out the window, maybe trying to ignore the sudden awkwardness between us.

But I can't ignore it. And so I drop my fork to the plate with a clang.

"Is everything okay?" he asks.

I shake my head, feeling my face flash hot before I can even get the words out. "I was just kind of wondering . . ."

"Yeah?"

"I was just kind of wondering," I repeat. "How long will I have to wait before you touch me again?"

Ben stares at me for several seconds without saying anything.

And then he touches me.

His fingers glide along my forearm and then clasp my wrist, sending an electric current down my back. He takes in a long full breath to keep himself in check. Still, his forehead is sweating, and he's shaking all over.

He stares down at our hands, clasped together like two parts of a ceramic mold. "I should probably get you home," he says, finally letting go. "It's been a long day, hasn't it?"

I agree, secretly wishing the day could be longer.

36

JT'S THE FOLLOWING MORNING, about twenty minutes before the warning bell, and I'm actually relieved to be in school.

I don't think Mom slept at all last night. And neither did I. While she was busy pacing back and forth in the kitchen, drinking cup after cup of her dandelion tea, I lay in bed with my light on and the door open a crack, completely freaked out.

At breakfast, I tried to ask Mom about Aunt Alexia, but she wasn't up for talking. Nor was Dad. Both just sort of sat at the table, staring off into space—Dad with his coffee and Mom with more tea. Neither mentioned anything about me wanting to talk last night.

Neither ever noticed that I sneaked away.

The corridors at school are eerily deserted this morning. I look out my homeroom window, curious about whether there's been a fire drill, expecting to see rows of students lined up in the parking lot. Instead, there are swarms of people hanging around by the football field. And so I head out there, too, not quite prepared for what I see.

Polly Piranha, the school's mascot, has once again been vandalized. Someone's changed the words that float above her fins from *Freetown High, Home of the Piranhas* to *Freetown High, Home of the Convicted Murderer*.

I look around for Ben, wondering if he's seen it. Meanwhile, a group of freshman boys is practically in stitches on the sideline. And they're not the only ones. People are laughing. Boys are high-fiving. Groups of girls are giggling between whispers.

I turn to go back inside when I spot a mob of people crowded around a freshman girl. She looks upset. Her face is red, and there are tears streaming down her cheeks. I get close so I can listen in. They're asking her questions about Ben—about the notes he's supposedly left on her locker, the way he's been following her around, and how he's allegedly been staring her down in history class.

"I don't know what I'm going to do," she says, tucking her fists into the pockets of her coat.

I move to the front of the crowd, until the girl and I are face to face.

"*What?*" she asks, giving me the once-over.

"Is your name Debbie?" I ask.

"Who wants to know?"

"I do," I say, taking a step closer.

She shuffles her feet and continues to study me; her deep brown eyes look me up and down.

I hand her a tissue from my bag. "Are you Debbie Marcus?" I ask.

She takes the tissue and wipes her face. There's a spray of freckles across the bridge of her nose. "Yeah," she says, finally.

"Well, then, can we talk a minute . . . over there?" I gesture to a spot behind a row of parked cars.

Debbie tucks her curly auburn locks behind her ears and then returns her hands to her pockets. "I guess so," she says, still sniffling.

We move away from the crowd, making sure no one follows.

"Is it true what I've been hearing?" I ask once we're behind the school van.

"If you're referring to the way Ben Carter's been harassing me, the answer is yes."

"Can you be a bit more specific?"

"About the harassment?"

I nod, noticing that her neck is all blotchy with hives.

"It all started in history class," she says. "He kept staring at me, like he was trying to psych me out."

"Did he touch you?"

"Touch me?" She cocks her head, visibly confused.

"I mean, did he grab you, or bump into you in any weird way?"

She looks back at me, completely puzzled. "He keeps his distance. He has some bizarro phobia, you know."

I manage a nod.

"But that doesn't keep him from watching me," she continues. "It doesn't keep him from leaving notes on my locker, or following me home."

"He followed you home?"

She nods. "A friend of mine spotted him sitting in the bushes across the street from my house."

"Did you do anything about it?"

"Of course I did. I told my parents; they called the school; my dad consulted a lawyer."

"And?"

"And what's it to you?" she asks, her lips bunching up. "Why are you asking me all this?"

"I'm just trying to figure things out." I look back toward the sign—and the word *Murderer*.

"What's there to figure out? The guy murdered his girlfriend."

"He wasn't found guilty."

"Because the judicial system is stupid. The police told my dad there's nothing we can do about him—that he has rights, that there's nothing illegal about looking at someone or even watching their house."

"You called the police?" I ask, remembering how Ben suggested that I do the same.

"Well, yeah, we called them. He was hiding in the bushes," she reminds me.

"Did you actually see him?"

"I didn't have to." She shrugs. "My friend saw him. She said he didn't even try to hide the fact that he was there. He just sort of sat there, huddled up, watching her watch him, like part of him enjoyed it. Like he didn't even care about getting caught."

"And, so, *did* you catch him? Did you go out there?"

"My dad went out, but Ben was already gone. You could totally tell where he was hiding, though. My neighbor's bush was all mangled and broken. Apparently not evidence enough, though, even *with* my friend's word. He has to do something *big* for the police take us seriously."

"Something big?"

"Be careful," she warns me. "And watch your back, if you know what I mean." She peers over my shoulder, where a group of onlookers is forming.

"No." I take a step closer. "What do you mean?"

"I can't talk right now," she says, superconscious of the crowd. "But if you don't believe me about what's going on, just check this out." She pulls a note from her coat pocket and hands it to me. "It was taped up on my locker this morning."

I unfold it and stare down at the message. The words *You're Next!* are scribbled across the page in black ink.

37

*B*EFORE I GO BACK INSIDE, I spot Kimmie and
Wes sitting outside in the courtyard across the
lawn. Kimmie waves, and I head over to join
them, slightly taken aback by her outfit du jour. There's a
pink studded choker fastened around her neck. An actual
dog leash is attached to it, which in turn hooks on to her
matching pink gumball ring.

"It's from my Princess S-and-M line," she explains.

"Where were you last night?" I ask.

"Sorry," she says. "After I got back from your house,
I got into a huge fight with my parents for going out
at all. They sequestered me in my bedroom sans cell
phone."

"What about the library?"

"Um, what library?"

"Your mom said that's where you went."

Kimmie shakes her head. "I was home. I have the

designs to prove it—a strappy dress with beaded fringe and leather detail. I call it Roaring Twenties Meets Today's Vampy Vixen."

"Or you could simply call it ugly," Wes suggests.

"I bet she just said that so she wouldn't have to come get me in my room," Kimmie continues. "The woman was a raving loony last night."

"And I have the bite marks to prove it," Wes jokes.

"I guess . . ." I mutter, not knowing what else to say— or what to believe.

"This school is lame," Wes says. "I mean, check it out." He gestures toward the sign with his Slurpee. "They didn't even spell *murderer* right."

"Um, yes they did," Kimmie says.

Wes sips thoughtfully and takes another look, trying to figure it out.

"Has Snell been out here?" I ask.

"Principal *Smell*," he says, "has yet to make an appearance."

"But I'm sure he's crapping himself as we speak," Kimmie says. "Rumor has it a reporter for the *Tribune* was here earlier. Apparently they already nabbed a photo op. Prepare to see it on the front page tomorrow."

"With a bunch of cheesy freshman posing in front of it," Wes says.

"Speaking of freshmen," I say, "I spoke to that Debbie girl."

"The one who's supposedly on Ben's butcher list?" Wes asks.

I nod reluctantly and then fill them in on what she said, including about the note.

"Just a note?" Kimmie asks. "No creepy snapshots of her hanging around the school?"

"No pj's left on her windowsill?" Wes adds.

"The note didn't look anything like the ones I got," I say. "It actually looked more like the one on Ben's locker. They were both written on scraps of paper in regular black ink."

"So, what does that prove?" Wes asks.

"Maybe hers is a joke, but mine isn't." I shrug.

"I don't know," Wes says. "It seems pretty weird that Ben's been hanging around you both."

"And randomly shows up at both of your houses when you least expect it," Kimmie adds.

"Not to mention the notes, the stares, the way he's always touching you," Wes says.

"But he doesn't touch *her*," I pipe up, as though that's supposed to defend him.

"Oh my god!" Kimmie squeals, spotting John Kenneally in the crowd. She straightens out the hem of her poofy skirt. "Is he coming over here? How do I look?"

"How can you even be interested in him?" I ask.

"Are you blind?"

"Are *you*? Did you not see the way he acted in the cafeteria the other day—how he dumped a bowl of soup over Ben's head?"

"Okay, no comment." She exchanges a look with Wes—complete with bulging eyes and raised eyebrows.

171

"Right," Wes says. "Let's talk about something a bit safer, shall we?"

"Forget it," I say, getting up from the table.

"Camelia!" Kimmie squawks. "Don't be like that."

"Like what?" I snap. "How can you be attracted to someone so openly cruel?"

"And how can *you* can be attracted to someone so completely creepy?"

I look away, not knowing what to say, deciding not to tell them about my mirror, the shredded pj's, or my night out with Ben.

"Seriously," she continues, "you can't honestly tell me this Sour Patch Kids mood of yours is all because I happen to think John's hot."

I shrug, suspecting she's right—that it has more to do with who I can trust. I glance back in the direction of the sign and, as if by fate, Ben's motorcycle comes pulling into the parking lot.

"Shit, meet fan," Wes says, somewhat under his breath.

Ben parks his bike and then sees the sign. Meanwhile, everyone is staring right at him, waiting for his response.

I clench my teeth, hoping he won't let it bother him, that he'll take the proverbial high road and let it roll right off his back. But instead he takes his helmet and whips it at the sign, then hops back on his bike and revs up the engine so loud I feel my insides explode.

He peels out of the parking lot, and it's quiet for several moments—there's just the hum of his engine as it continues down the street.

38

HE DAY IS A COMPLETE AND TOTAL bust, one
I never should have gotten out of bed for. Ben
doesn't come back to school. Kimmie and I don't
really talk much. The principal calls for an impromptu
assembly, where he lectures about the Polly Piranha van-
dalism, the havoc wreaked since the very first day of school,
and the way the reputation of our high school has been seriously damaged (the real impetus for the assembly). Top all
of that off with the Sweat-man's brilliant idea of throwing
a near-impossible pop quiz, and I'm an emotional wreck.

And so, in spite of how weird things got between
Spencer and me in school the other day, I head to work
early, hoping that the sensation of sticky red clay against
my cold and clammy fingertips will help me relax and put
things in perspective. The good thing is that Spencer isn't
even there when I arrive. I've got the entire studio to
myself.

I line up all my tools, grab my board, and unwrap the piece I started, removing the plastic tarp and damp paper towels—essentials that keep the clay from hardening. With my eyes closed, I spend several moments just breathing into the clay, trying to block out any stray thoughts, to focus instead on my fingers as they smooth over bumps and glide across cracks.

After several minutes, I feel the clay begin to take shape beneath my fingertips. My eyes still closed, I prod a little further, creating what feels like a sharp angle extending up from a boxlike base. I open my eyes to see what it looks like.

Spencer's there. He's standing just a few feet away.

I let out a gasp and take a step back, knocking a stack of cups off the shelf behind me.

"I didn't mean to startle you," he says. "You just looked so inspired. I didn't want to interrupt."

"Where did you come from?" I ask, looking toward the door, knowing I would have heard the bells jingle if he'd just come in.

"I was downstairs pulling molds." He takes a step closer to view my piece. "What are you working on?"

"Something with a pulse, I hope."

Spencer smiles and runs a hand through his dark hair. "I had a feeling you were bothered by that."

I shrug and look down at my piece, anxious to see what's become of it. There's a rectangular form at the bottom, with a smaller version of the same on top—sort of like a car, minus the wheels.

"I only said that to push you deeper," he says. "You have a lot of talent, but sometimes I think you take the easy way out. You don't take the time to examine the guts."

The guts?

"Dig a little," he continues. "Search. Examine. Sculpt from the inside out, and not the other way around. Don't be afraid to screw up along the way."

"I screw up plenty," I tell him, still looking at my lame-o car figure.

"Good." His smile morphs into a smirk. "You need to screw up to learn. You need to experience to create greatness. It's not just about bowls, you know." He takes another step, as if he wants to get an even closer glimpse of the angles of my piece, but instead he's looking at me, his face just inches from mine now. "It's good to see you experimenting. I can't wait to see what comes of it."

"Yeah," I say, noticing the razor cut on his neck. "Me, too."

"And that invitation's still open if you ever want to talk."

I nod, suddenly feeling as if the walls are closing in. I try to move away, but between the shelf and Spencer I'm totally pinned.

A moment later, I hear the door jangle open. Spencer moves to pick up the cups that fell off the shelf, and then turns to see who's here.

It's Matt, and I couldn't be happier to see him.

Holding two cups of coffee, he approaches cautiously, glancing back and forth between Spencer and me, like maybe he thinks he's interrupting something.

"Come on in," I tell him.

He slides a cup of coffee across the table at me—since my hands are covered in clay. "I was just in the area." He looks back at Spencer. "I thought I'd say hi."

"I'm glad you did." I smile wide, hoping Spencer gets the hint and heads back downstairs.

But instead he sticks around, introduces himself, and starts telling Matt how talented he thinks I am. "This girl is going places," Spencer says. Eventually, he turns and leaves us alone, and I'm able to regroup.

Matt looks particularly good today—sun-kissed hair, a charcoal gray sweatshirt to contrast with his glowing complexion, and a bit of golden stubble across his chin.

"Thanks for the coffee." I wipe my hands and take a sip, noticing the hazelnut flavor with just the right amount of sugar and milk. "You remembered how I take my coffee."

"It wasn't that long ago."

"Right," I say, remembering how our relationship actually started with coffee—with the two of us meeting up at Press & Grind, the coffee place downtown, every Thursday night to study.

"Those were some fun times," he says. His blue eyes beam right into mine. "Remember Philippe?"

I let out a giggle, recalling the wacko barista who used to juggle espresso cups and do magic tricks with cappuccino foam. "I wonder if he still works there."

"We should totally go check one day."

"That'd be fun," I say, hoping some of the awkwardness has finally lifted between us. It's just so weird how only three short weeks of dating can screw up what had been an otherwise perfectly good platonic relationship. I tried to explain that on one of our last dates—that things had worked better when it was just coffee, books, and entertaining baristas. But he didn't really get it, and I didn't know what else to say.

And what *could* I say? He was the quintessential perfect boyfriend—good-looking, called me all the time, bought me thoughtful little gifts, and remembered everything I told him. Kimmie thought I was verging on insanity, but breaking up with Matt was like having a really good cup of coffee—completely eye-opening and totally essential. I just wasn't ready for all that intensity. Not the way I am now.

I look down at my mound of clay, thinking about Ben—about the intensity I felt at his touch alone.

"So, what's up with your creepy boss?" Matt asks.

I shake my head, wondering where he went off to. I didn't hear him go back downstairs.

"Seems you have a lot of creepy guys in your life," he continues.

"Have you been talking to Kimmie?"

"Just a little." He smirks.

"Did she send you down here?"

"She's worried about you," he says. "And I guess I am, too."

"What did she say?"

He shrugs. "Stuff about that Ben guy—how he's hanging around you a lot."

I purse my lips, not surprised by her blabbing, but relieved that it seems she didn't say anything about the whole touching issue. "I can handle Ben."

"Are you sure? Because you know how I feel about that guy."

"I know what I'm doing."

"And what *are* you doing? I mean, the guy's developed quite a reputation for himself, don't you think?"

"You don't understand."

"Well, then make me understand."

I shake my head, unwilling to get into it—with my ex, of all people.

"Look, I'm not trying to piss you off," he continues. "I'm just looking out for you. Ex-boyfriends are allowed to do that, right?"

"I suppose," I grin.

"Well, suppose this," he says, all smirky again, "I'm always here if you need me."

"You know you really need to stop being so mean to me all the time," I joke. "People will start to talk."

"I like being mean to you," he smiles.

"Do you like being mean to Rena Maruso?" I ask, regretting it just as soon as the question comes out my mouth.

He takes another sip, clearly amused. The corners of his mouth turn upward, and he stares at me over the rim of his paper cup. "What if I said yes?"

"Then I'd be happy for you."

"And if I said no? That I much prefer torturing you?"

I feel my face get hot.

"Forget it," he says. "Don't answer that. Maybe I don't want to know."

"It was really sweet of you to stop by," I say, trying to fill the sudden and very awkward silence. "Thanks for the coffee."

"My pleasure." He turns away, leaving me somewhat hanging, even though a part of me doesn't want to know the answer either.

39

She royally betrayed me, but now it's my turn to make things right. Part of me wants to rip her in two. Another part wants to laugh out loud, knowing what I've got planned for her.

I felt that way in her room. I saw that lingerie still in its box. How ungrateful is that? And so I ripped the material to shreds.

I imagined it was her there, and then I angled my body over the clothes, teasing the fabric with the tip of my knife right before I slashed it up.

It felt good to do it, too. I started to laugh after it happened. I could barely even calm myself down. Everything just seemed funny all of a sudden. But then I saw what I did.

I saw the word Bitch on her mirror. And it even scared me.

I stood there, looking at everything I'd done. I didn't know if I should laugh some more or be sick. I started shaking. But then I remembered that this is what she wants, that she's such a selfish bitch, and that she doesn't know what's good for her, not like I do.

THE REMAINDER OF MY DAY at Knead is pretty uneventful. While Spencer spends most of my shift pulling molds downstairs, I use my time setting up for classes, firing a bunch of greenware, and trying to decide what to do.

This whole Debbie scenario has got me completely on edge, especially considering the timing of things. I mean, just when I decide to trust Ben, something like this happens, that makes me question everything all over again.

After work, I take a bus to the stop at the end of our street, despite Spencer's offer to drop me off. But when I get to my house it's completely dark. It seems my parents aren't home yet, even though it's after eight o'clock.

Not knowing where else to go, and feeling stupid for considering hanging out at one of my neighbors' houses, I unlock the door and switch on some lights. I tell myself everything will be fine, even though my stomach is in knots.

In my room, I glance toward the mirror. For a split second, I see the red letters splotched across my face, but when I blink, they're gone.

I continue around the house, making sure that all the doors and windows are locked. I even go down to the basement, passing by my pottery station and noticing the jump rope–like worm I sculpted the other day; I'm surprised I forgot to clean it up.

A second later, the phone rings, startling me. I decide to ignore it and head back upstairs to check out the bathroom. My dad's tacked some plastic up over the broken window, but someone could easily break through it.

I grab a razor from the shelf and look over my shoulder. At the same moment a shadow moves across the wall. I let out a gasp and peer down the hallway in both directions. There's nothing there. Meanwhile the phone continues to ring. It's like someone keeps calling back because they know I'm home.

Alone.

I move into the kitchen and check the answering machine, but no one's left a message.

Completely unnerved, I drop the razor on the counter and pick up the receiver, hoping that it's my parents. I click the phone on and mumble a hello, but no one answers. It's just quiet on the other end, like someone's listening in.

"Hello?" I repeat, a little louder this time.

Still nothing. I hang up, feeling my skin ice over.

I click the phone back on to leave it off the hook and

then grab my cell phone from my bag, but unfortunately I can't get a signal.

I move toward the window, hoping that will help. I catch a glimpse of a note tacked up on the fridge. It's from my mom, along with a twenty-dollar bill, instructing me to order a pizza from Raw. It seems she and my dad won't be home until late.

Still without a cell phone signal, I take a deep breath and sit on a stool, literally counting to ten, trying to reassure myself that everything will be okay, despite the buzzing sound of the phone off the hook and the racing of my pulse.

After several seconds, the phone finally stops, and I'm able to calm down, but my stomach rumbles, and my head feels foggy. I reluctantly click the phone back on and peer up at the list of take-out numbers by the fridge, realizing I haven't eaten anything since breakfast. The number for Raw is highlighted in bright melon pink, but instead I order a good old-fashioned cheese-and-mushroom from the pizza shop downtown, and then sit perched on the living room sofa waiting for it to arrive.

Still holding the phone in my hand, I'm tempted to give Kimmie a call. A moment later it rings—the sound cuts through my bones. I click the receiver on and place it up to my ear.

"Camelia?" a male voice says before I can speak.

"Who's this?"

"It's me." The voice brightens. "Ben."

My heart tightens, and my stomach twists.

"Did you call before?" I ask.

"Yeah, but the line was busy. I would have tried your cell, but you didn't give me the number."

"How did you know I was home?"

"I didn't. I just thought I'd give it a shot."

"But I just got here," I say. "How did you know the precise time to call me?"

"Are you okay?" he asks.

"Maybe I should be asking you the same. You never made it back to school today."

"Don't worry about me."

"We really need to talk," I say, trying to be brave.

"About what?"

"Not over the phone."

"Are you alone?"

"No," I lie.

"Good. Your parents are there?"

I look out the living room window, noticing that the streetlamp in front of our house is still out. It seems my neighbors aren't around, either. The porch lights across the street and next door are all off.

"Camelia?"

"I'm here."

"What's wrong?" he asks.

I grab an afghan from the foot of the sofa and drape it over me, to try and take the chill off.

"You're alone, aren't you?" he says, his voice is barely above a whisper.

I reach up to yank the curtains closed and then check

around the room, making sure no one can see me through any other window.

"I'm coming over," he continues. "You don't sound right."

"I'm fine," I say, to reassure him.

It's quiet on the other end for several seconds, but then he tells me he's coming over anyway. "I'll be there soon," he says.

I hang up, opting not to argue, but instead to go with my gut, especially since there's so much I need to ask him about.

A few seconds later, the phone rings again. "Hello?"

No one answers, but I can tell someone's there. I can hear breathing on the other end, followed by a weird scratching sound. "Hello?"

"Don't forget the mailbox," a voice whispers finally, sending chills straight down my back.

"Excuse me?"

"The mailbox," he hisses. "You forgot to check it on the way in."

"Who is this?" I move to a corner window and peek out from behind the curtain. But I don't see anyone.

"Good things come to those who wait," he says, his voice softening again. "I've waited for you. Now it's your turn."

"Who is this?" I shout.

"Luckily, you won't have to wait too long." He hangs up.

The receiver clutched in my hand, I go to the door. Meanwhile, the phone starts ringing again. I ignore it and peer through the peephole. The mailbox flag is in the up position.

41

INSTEAD OF CHECKING THE MAILBOX, I end up pacing across the living room floor, trying to decide whether or not to call my parents and ask them to come home. I'm dialing my dad's number when I hear a car door slam in front of the house.

A second later, there's a knock on the door—a hard-fisted bang, followed by the sound of the doorbell ringing. Too afraid to go to the door, I grab a pottery bowl and position myself behind the buffet, away from the windows so no one can see me. Meanwhile the doorbell continues and so does the banging.

I take a deep breath, trying to stop the tightening sensation inside my chest.

The outer door swings open. The doorknob jiggles back and forth. I click the phone on, prepared to dial 911.

But then the banging stops—just like that. The outer

door closes, too. A few seconds later, I hear the car door slam again.

Slowly I move from behind the buffet to look out the window. A small dark car peels away with a screech.

But then the doorbell rings again.

Shaking, I walk toward the door.

"Camelia?" a male voice calls from just behind it.

I peer through the peephole. It's Ben. And he's holding a pizza.

I unlock the door and whisk it open, having completely forgotten I ordered dinner.

There's a huge grin across his face. "Did you order a large cheese with mushroom? You owe me fifteen bucks, by the way."

"You scared me."

"I can see that." He gestures toward the pottery bowl, still gripped in my hand.

The mailbox is in full view now, just behind him, with the flag pointed upward. I close my eyes a moment, still able to hear the caller's voice in my mind's ear, telling me to look inside.

"What is it?" Ben asks.

I motion to the mailbox.

"Do you want me to check?"

I shake my head and step outside, wondering if I'm being watched. But I don't see anyone, and nothing looks unusual.

"What's wrong?" He takes a step closer to me.

I inhale the cool night air and let it filter out slowly in

one long and visible puff. Aside from the screeching of Davis Miller's electric guitar at the end of the street, it's eerily quiet. I glance around, spotting Ben's motorcycle parked on the corner. "Did you just get here?"

He nods.

"Are you sure?" I ask, almost positive I would have heard the motor rumble his arrival.

"Why would I lie?"

"I don't know," I say, meeting his eye.

"Are you saying you don't trust me?" His dark eyes narrow.

I ignore the question and look away, back toward the mailbox. With trembling fingers I open it up.

There's a large manila envelope inside with my name written on the front. "Another photo," I say, recognizing the red lettering. I take the envelope, lead Ben inside, and then lock the door.

"Let me open it," he says. "If he recently left it, it may still have his energy. I might be able to sense something."

We sit opposite one another at the kitchen island. Ben brushes his fingers over the surface of the envelope.

"Do you feel anything?" I ask.

He closes his eyes to concentrate. The muscles in his forearms pulse. "Soon," he whispers, letting out a giant breath.

"Soon what?"

Instead of answering, he opens the flap and reaches inside. He pulls out a bunch of cut-up photos. I take a closer look, noticing how they appear to be part of a whole.

Ben flips through them, running his fingers over the edges.

"It's a puzzle, isn't it?" I say.

Ben spreads the pieces flat on the marble surface and begins to put the image together. The bright red letters scrawled across the photo's surface makes it easier. It's only a matter of seconds before the message becomes clear.

"Time's almost up," I whisper, reading the words aloud.

It's a picture of me glancing down at my watch. "It was taken today," I say, noting that my clothes and hair are the same. "On my way to Knead."

Ben turns to me. A strand of his dark, wavy hair falls into his eyes. "I'm not going to let anything happen to you," he says.

"Promise?"

He reaches for my hand, but then stops just shy of it. His fingers tremble, like he wants to touch me but can't.

Please, I scream inside my head. There's an aching inside me so strong my head feels suddenly dizzy.

Ben grazes my thumb with his finger. I wonder if he can read my mind—and this is all he can manage for now. "I promise," he says. "But right now we need to keep focused."

"Right," I agree, glancing back at the photo and the message scribbled across it. "Because there isn't much time."

And my life depends on it.

42

EN AND I SPEND THE next full hour discussing the photo and the phone call I got earlier.

"He's definitely close." Ben presses a piece of the photo between two fingers and looks toward the kitchen window, but the blind's already drawn.

"I think it's time to call the police," I say.

Ben shakes his head and presses harder, nearly mangling the piece. "I've had it with police."

"Because of before?" I ask.

"Because of right now." He drops the photo piece and swivels on his stool to face me. "They gave me a warning."

"The police?"

He nods. "That Debbie girl told them I've been following her."

"And they believe her?"

Ben shrugs. "I don't know what they believe, but they

started asking me all these questions—where I've been at certain times, who I hang around with, and what I do when I'm alone."

"And what did you tell them?"

"The truth. What else could I tell them?"

"I talked to Debbie," I say, eager for the truth myself.

Ben nods, seemingly unsurprised.

"She really believes it," I continue. "She really thinks you want to hurt her."

"I know. I've heard it."

But, still, he doesn't deny it.

It's quiet between us for several moments—just the hum of the refrigerator and the clicking of the second hand from the cat-shaped kitchen clock.

"So, why would she say all that?" I ask, cutting through the silence.

Ben inches in a little closer. His clothes smell like burning leaves. "I know it's a lot to ask, but you have to trust me."

"She said you guys are in history class together."

"And so, what does that prove? I'm not after Debbie."

"Then who *are* you after?"

"Nobody." He shakes his head.

"So touch me again." I slide my hand toward his. "And tell me when all of this is going to end."

Ben eyes my hand, clearly tempted, but then he swivels away.

"What's wrong?"

"It's complicated."

"What is? I mean, we've already been through this. You're not going to hurt me."

"How do you know?" He runs his fingers through his hair in frustration.

"I *don't* know," I sigh. "But if you don't even try, then why did you bother telling me about your touch powers? Time's almost up." I gesture toward the photo. "And that could be me."

"I know." His jaw is visibly tense. "But you don't understand."

"Then make me understand. Tell me what's going on inside your head."

"I'm haunted by her," he whispers.

"You mean Julie?"

He nods. "I keep seeing her face. I keep seeing her fall off that cliff."

"It was an accident," I remind him.

Ben hikes up his sleeves as if he's suddenly hot, revealing the narrow gash that runs up his forearm.

"Is that where you got your scar?" I ask.

He nods and looks down at it. "It's like a permanent reminder of what happened. After she fell, I tried to climb down the cliff—to get to her—but I ended up tearing my arm open on a jagged rock."

"Was that incident the first time you sensed stuff?"

He shakes his head and tugs his sleeves back down. "But before that it was only small stuff. I'd bump someone's shoulder and know their car would get a flat, or I'd shake someone's hand and picture what they'd be having for dinner that night. At first I thought it was coincidence, but then it got kind of obvious—I'd be able to predict stuff."

"Did you ever use that to your advantage?"

"I never wanted to use it, period. Plus, this touching thing . . . it isn't always predictable. I can't always sense what I want to. I mean, I can try—I can concentrate really hard. But, like, with you, for example, sometimes I'll sense danger, and other times I'll feel something else entirely."

"Like what?"

He stares at me as if he doesn't want to say. "I did research on psychometry when the symptoms first started," he segues. "I needed to know what was happening to me, why I was able to see such vivid details by merely touching someone—like with Julie."

I look away tempted to remind him that I'm not her. But then I feel it—he swallows my hand up in his. And then he slides off his stool and takes a step forward, so close that my face is level with his chest.

"What are you thinking?" he asks. The cotton of his sweatshirt presses against my cheek with each breath.

"*You tell me,*" I say, noticing how that same breath deepens and becomes rhythmic, as if he's trying his best to stay in control.

He grips me tighter, and threads his fingers through mine.

"Do you feel anything?" I ask.

He meets my eyes, just watching me for several

194

seconds without saying anything. "You're a control freak, aren't you?"

"That's what you sense?"

"It's what I observe. You like to have things in order. You like everything all planned out. Am I right?"

My mouth trembles, and I manage a nod.

Meanwhile, Ben edges closer. His leg grazes my thigh. "So, what do you do about things beyond your control?" he asks.

"Like what?"

His hand clenches mine harder, in a tightening pressure that nearly makes me lose my breath. "Like whether or not it's going to rain tomorrow, or whether I'm going to kiss you right now."

I open my mouth to speak—to tell him he'll have to find out for himself—but then he moves in to kiss me anyway.

A moment later, the front door swings open with a bang.

He jumps back and releases my hand.

"Camelia, are you home?" my dad calls.

Ben scurries to grab the pieces of photo. He feeds them inside the envelope, then stashes it up the back of his sweatshirt.

A second later, my parents come into the kitchen. They look back and forth between Ben and me, waiting for some explanation, but I don't even know what just happened myself.

Ben introduces himself as my lab partner from school.

My mother extends her hand for a shake. Ben eyes it, but he doesn't move.

Her face furrowed, Mom looks at Dad and then at me.

At the same moment, Ben quickly shakes her hand—their fingers barely touch—and then tells us he has to go.

43

I CAN'T SLEEP.

It's almost midnight, and I'm lying awake in bed, trying my best to put the events of the night behind me and get a little rest.

But it isn't working.

After Ben left, my mother sat me down for a talk. And while I thought she'd at least mention Ben's visit and his weird handshake, his name never even came up.

"Where did you and Dad go tonight?" I asked, noticing how she couldn't even look at me. Her skin was all blotchy, and her normally kinky curls were slicked back into a tight knot.

After several sips of tea and countless yoga breaths, she finally opened up, telling me how she and Dad went to the hospital today intending to visit Aunt Alexia, but how once there my mother couldn't even bring herself to step inside.

"I couldn't face her," she said. "I couldn't look her in the eye."

I scooted in closer to pat her back. "Why is she even in there?"

With a pillow clutched over her middle, my mother told me that Aunt Alexia tried to kill herself again (for the fourth time, to be exact).

"Is she going to be all right?"

Instead of answering, Mom started crying, and so dad scooped her up and carried her off to their bedroom.

And meanwhile I went off to mine.

I roll over in bed, looking for my stuffed polar bear, but it isn't burrowed under my covers or stashed under my mound of pillows. I let out a sigh and gaze toward the window.

The moon is swollen and stirring tonight—just like me. My body feels bruised, and I can't seem to stifle this tugging sensation inside me. I pull the covers up to my chin only to find that they make me feel smothered. And so I sit up in bed, wishing I were outside, to feel the velvety night air over my skin and allow its darkness to swallow me whole.

I look toward my bedroom door. My mother is still sobbing—I can hear her in the bedroom across the hall. I can hear my dad, too. He tells her everything will be okay. I wonder if he really believes it.

The moon casts a strip of light across my bed, cutting it in two. Slowly I get up and move to the window. I pull up the screen, and a salty breeze blows through, smelling like the sea, reminding me of Ben.

I grab my cell phone and start to call him, but I'm still not getting a signal, and so, without even thinking, I reach for my jacket and crawl outside, hoping that will make a difference. Finally, the call goes through.

"Camelia?" He answers on the first ring.

Standing at the front of my house, I clutch the phone against my ear, not even knowing what to say.

"Where are you?" he asks, not even asking for explanation.

"Outside," I reply, trying to be mysterious. The light of the moon illuminates a puddle on the street. "And you?"

"Same," he whispers.

"For real?"

"I couldn't sleep. I needed some air."

My pulse quickens, and my blood stirs. It feels like there's a fire inside me. I look back toward my bedroom window, unwilling to go in just yet. "Will you come get me?" I ask.

"I was hoping you'd say that."

"Really?"

"Really," he says, "because I'm already on my way."

He clicks the phone off. A few minutes later, I hear the sound of his motorcycle from several streets away. It moves closer, getting louder and filling my head with a numbing buzz.

I walk to the edge of the street, finally able to see him. He pulls over, hands me his helmet, and tells me to hop on.

44

I TELL BEN TO TAKE US TO KNEAD; it's after hours, but I have the key. He pulls his bike around to the back, and I lead him to the rear entrance.

"Are you sure this is okay?" he asks, sensing my mounting anxiety.

I nod, reminding myself that Spencer said I could come here anytime, that this is no big deal, and that we probably won't stay for more than a few minutes.

My fingers shake just trying to get the key into the lock. Finally it clicks, and I open the door.

"Is that turpentine?" he asks, noticing the smell.

I nod and flick on the light, then proceed to give him the grand tour. I point out shelves full of paints, glazes, and greenware; bins full of slip, tools, and decals—probably explaining way more than he's interested in. I'm just so completely nervous right now, just being here. Alone with him.

"Are you sure you won't get in trouble?" he asks.

"I'm sure," I say, leading him into the studio. The floor creaks beneath our steps.

"Well, then, can I see your stuff?"

I point out several bowls I've made as models for the classes, suddenly realizing how similar they all look—all versions of the same thing.

"And what are you working on now?" he asks.

I glance over at the tarp-covered piece that sits in the corner.

Ben follows my gaze, then goes over to look more closely. "This one?" he asks, trying to sneak a peek.

I nod, hesitant to show him, but then I lift off the plastic covering and remove the paper towels. The car-shaped piece sits slumped against the board, just as sad-looking as it was on the day I sculpted it. "It's a work in progress," I tell him.

"Cool."

"Maybe. I'm not really sure what it is yet. I was kind of just going with my gut—if that makes any sense."

"It actually makes perfect sense." He spends several moments looking at it from different angles, as if he can see something I can't. "It's really something," he says.

"Something," I smile. "I think that would be a good assessment."

"That's not what I meant."

I venture to look at his face, conscious that there's way more going on here than just my sucky sculpture.

Ben stares right back at me. His jaw tightens, and he presses his lips together. "Can I ask you something?"

"Sure," I say, trying to stay composed.

"Why did you want me to pick you up? I mean, I'm glad you did, don't get me wrong. I'm just curious."

I cover my piece back up, not knowing how to answer.

"Did it have anything to do with your mom?" he asks.

"What about her?"

"I touched her, remember?"

My mind races as I imagine what he might know—that he was able to sense anything at all.

"There was an accident," he continues. "It involved someone really close to your mom, like a sister or a close friend."

"You were able to sense that from a handshake?"

"Am I right? Is she okay?"

"My mom or my aunt?"

"Both."

I look down at my tarp-covered piece, thinking about the last time my mother was this depressed. "It seems my aunt will be okay. As for my mother, I honestly don't know."

"She needs to stop blaming herself for whatever happened. It wasn't her fault."

"Maybe you should take your own advice," I say, looking back at him.

"Who says I blame myself?"

"I do. And I don't even need to touch you to know it."

202

"Maybe I just wish I could go back and make things right."

"Will helping me make things right? Will it help ease some of the guilt?"

"It isn't the only reason I want to help you. I mean, maybe it started out that way, but now, after getting to know you, I need to help you."

"Really?" My voice is shaky.

"Really," he says, moving closer. Our faces are just a kiss apart.

I try to touch his scar, but he pulls away before I can.

"I'm sorry," he says, turning away so I can't see his face or how runny his eyes look.

"Not all touch is bad, you know." I open a box of fresh red clay, slice off a nice, thick chunk, and then set it down on a board in front of him.

"What's that for?" he asks.

"You said you wanted to learn sculpture, didn't you?"

Ben nods hesitantly and takes the hunk of clay. Slowly, he palms the surface, but it's clear he doesn't know what to do.

"It isn't going to bite," I say, filling a cup with some water from the sink. I dip a sponge inside the cup and then squeeze some droplets of water over his fingers to help him dampen the clay. "You'll need to keep saturating your work so it doesn't dry out."

He pushes at the clay with his fingertips, but it's almost as if he won't let go—as if he's holding a big part of himself back.

"Here," I say, rolling his sleeves up to his elbows. "Try to get into it."

"I don't know." He shakes his head. "Maybe sculpture's not my thing."

"Just give it a chance." I roll my sleeves up, too, and then gently place my hands over his. Ben flinches at first. The veins in his arms tense. But then I guide my fingers over his, helping him knead the clay. Together, we roll it out beneath our palms, and eventually his fingers relax.

Ben's breath is slow and rhythmic, like he's trying his best to concentrate.

"You won't hurt me," I say, sliding my hand up his forearm, then touching his scar. My fingers run over it, making the hairs on his arm pasty and wet.

Ben locks eyes with me.

"Is this too much?" I ask, conscious of my breathing, too, and how my heart is beating extra fast.

Ben opens his mouth to say something, but instead he stays quiet, allowing me to continue guiding his hands over the clay. Our fingers thread themselves together and push against the mound's surface, creating notches and dents. After several minutes we sculpt what appears to be a pear-shaped pinecone.

"Not bad," I say, noting the symmetry. "What do you think?"

Ben faces me. His eyes bore into mine, like he has something important to say.

"What's wrong?" I ask. "Did you sense something I should know about?"

He reaches out to touch me. His skin is moist and slippery against mine. "Shhh . . ." he says, concentrating. He glides his palms over my forearms and then snakes them up toward my shoulders, beneath my sleeves.

My pulse is racing. My stomach starts tumbling. Ben brushes his hand against my cheek.

I close my eyes and feel his fingers at the nape of my neck. He pulls me even closer, and my cheek touches his chin.

"Relax," he whispers into my ear.

And then he kisses me. His clay-covered fingers slide up the back of my T-shirt, against my skin, and turn my insides to mush.

I cup Ben's face in my hands and kiss him back, feeling his grip at my forearms again—the gritty feeling of his hands clenching at my wrists. "Is this getting too intense for you?" I ask, once the kiss breaks.

He shakes his head and slides our work board to the side, lifts me up and sits me down on top of the table. His waist presses against my thighs.

"Is this okay?" he whispers in my ear. His breath is hot and thick.

I manage a nod, and then we end up kissing for another full hour—until the clay dries up and dusts off our skin.

Until my head feels woozy and I can barely stand up straight.

45

AFTER BEN DROPS ME OFF, I lie awake in my bed, wondering if the night really happened or if it was just a dream.

I know that sounds sort of crazy, and normally I'd laugh if Kimmie or someone else said anything even remotely similar, but if it weren't for the tingling that still lingers on my lips or the pure electric current pulsing through my veins, I'd swear tonight was one big fantasy created by my subconscious. That's how amazing our evening was.

At the breakfast table, Dad is all pastry and orange juice. He's got a whole spread going, complete with sugar-coated strawberries, gluten-containing fritters, and a store-bought coffee cake that lists partially hydrogenated oil as one of its key ingredients. He's obviously trying to overcompensate for Mom's absence this morning. She's still in bed. When I passed by her room earlier, the covers were drawn up over her shoulders, and she refused to talk.

"She just needs a little space right now," Dad says when I ask.

"What about work?"

He sits down across from me at the island and takes a sip of coffee. "Someone's taking over her classes for the next couple of days."

"For the next couple of days or the next couple of weeks?"

He gives me a sharp look, but instead of answering, he keeps things light by asking about the cafeteria food at school and then handing me an extra five bucks for lunch.

"So, what are we going to do about it?" I ask.

"About Mom?" he asks, like I need to clarify. "We're going to give her a little space."

"But what if she doesn't *need* space?"

Dad clears his throat. "I know you mean well, but this is really between your mother and her sister."

"Aunt Alexia," I say correcting him, though it's weird to even call her that. The last time I saw her was when I was in preschool—at least that's what I'm told.

Dad clanks his mug against the granite counter in an effort to maintain his ground. "You really don't know anything about it."

"Well, I know that blaming yourself for stuff that happened forty years ago isn't the answer, either. I mean, do you honestly think it's Mom's fault that Grandma hated Alexia so much?"

"That's not why your mom blames herself."

"I know," I say, confident that it has more to do with the fact that, growing up, Mom did nothing to protect her little sister. According to Mom, Grandma treated Alexia with nothing but hatred, blaming Alexia's birth for her husband's leaving her. Meanwhile, my mom was loved and indulged, often as a way to make Alexia feel even more unwanted.

"It isn't Mom's fault that Aunt Alexia is having all these problems."

"Shhh . . ." Dad gestures toward the hallway. Their bedroom door is open a crack. "I honestly don't know what the answer is," he says, lowering his voice.

"Me, neither, but I do know that living in the past only messes up your present. Mom needs to deal with her demons and move on and stop living a life of guilt."

Dad smiles and stirs his coffee, even though it's black. "You sound like you know what you're talking about."

"I do," I say, thinking about Ben.

"So, how do we help her demon-deal?"

"For one, she needs to talk with her sister."

"And for two, I need to make a little more time so that *we* can talk." He clinks his mug against my juice glass. "I'm sorry I've been so preoccupied lately."

"It's okay," I say, almost tempted to tell him everything that's been going on.

Instead we make plans to talk over dinner—a long-overdue trip to Taco Bell for chips and chalupas—and then I head off to school.

It's barely eight in the morning, and the hallways are

already buzzing. I pass by the groups of cliques huddled in conversation, wondering what they're talking about and why they're staring right at me.

I see Matt at his locker, and he waves me over.

"What's going on?" I ask, noticing Davis Miller standing with a bunch of his band cohorts. They point in my direction.

"Haven't you heard?" Matt slams his locker door shut.

I shake my head, spotting a group of girls all teary-eyed in the corner. Senora Lynch is trying to console them.

"Debbie Marcus is in a coma," he says. "It happened last night."

"*What?*"

"It's true. Apparently she was walking home—late, like around one thirty or two in the morning—and someone plowed right into her."

"*Someone*, or a car?"

"A motorcycle, to be exact. At least that's what everybody's saying."

"So, they think it was Ben."

Matt shrugs. "Nobody else was after her."

"Wait," I say, shaking my head, knowing that it was around one or one thirty when Ben dropped me off at home. "Where did it happen?"

"Columbus Street—not far from your house. Why? Do you know something?"

"No," I lie, feeling my neck get hot. I take a deep breath and peer down the hallway, catching at least six different cliques all looking this way. "What's going on?"

"They think you're next."

"*What?*" My heart clenches, and my head fuzzes over.

"Camelia?" Matt takes a step closer and touches my forearm. "Do you need to sit down?"

I shake my head, trying to get a grip.

"You can't honestly tell me you're surprised, can you?" he asks.

"I just don't understand."

"This is all just what I heard," he assures me. "But the police are questioning him now."

"Him, as in Ben?"

"Well . . . yeah." He bites the inside of his cheek, like he can see how bothered I am—and like that bothers him, too.

"How do they know it was a motorcycle?" I ask. "Did anyone see it happen?"

"She told the police it was a motorcycle," Kimmie says, inserting herself into our conversation. "She also said Ben's name right before she fell into the coma."

"What was she doing walking around by herself at that hour?" I ask.

"People are saying she was supposed to be sleeping at her friend Manda's house," Matt explains. "But apparently there was some drama, and so Debbie decided to walk home, since her house is only five minutes away."

I shake my head again, completely confused. "It just doesn't make sense. How did this happen?"

"I think the question we should be asking ourselves is: what are *you* going to do about it?" Kimmie asks.

"*Me?*"

"Well, um, hello, he's stalking you, too."

"We're just worried about you," Matt says. He exchanges a look with Kimmie, like they've obviously discussed my welfare.

"Ben's not the one stalking me."

"Oh, yeah, and who told you that?" Kimmie asks. "*Ben?*"

"You don't know what you're talking about," I tell her.

"No," she snaps. "You don't. I'm just trying to be a good friend—unlike you."

"What's that supposed to mean?"

While Matt excuses himself, promising to talk to me later, Kimmie digs her fists deeper into the pockets of her dress.

"When was the last time you asked me about what *I'm* feeling, or what's going on in *my* life?" She continues by pointing out that I never inquired about the workshop she's applying to at the Fashion Institute, and that I haven't shown even a speck of concern about what's going on inside her house.

"You mean with your dad?" I ask, noticing the letter *K* patched at the hem of her dress, along with a black lipstick smudge—her trademark logo.

"Well, yeah, with my dad," she snaps. "I mean, he's been acting all twenty-something-frat-boy lately, and you haven't even asked me about it. And it's not just me," she continues, without missing a breath. "You haven't been supportive of Wes, either."

"*Wes?*"

She nods. "How come you never offered to play girlfriend in front of his dad?"

"I don't know," I say, feeling my chin shake.

"I don't know, either." She sighs. "And I really don't feel like fighting with you anymore, especially about Ben."

"I've had a lot on my plate," I say in my own defense.

"Which is why I've been so patient with you. It's also why I've indulged you with all your Ben talk."

"You don't understand about Ben," I say. "He was able to sense that time I got lost in the second grade. Remember . . . at recess?"

"Are you seriously kidding me?" She rolls her eyes. "*Everybody* at that school knew you were lost—they announced it over the loudspeaker. You think it would be totally unheard of for him to find out? This is a small town, Camelia. People talk."

I take a deep breath, my head spinning. It feels like I've been socked in the gut.

"Look," she continues, taking a step closer to meet my gaze, "I'm only going to say this once: I don't trust Ben. I don't trust the stories he's been feeding you. And neither does anyone else. One girl is dead, another is in a coma. What's going to happen to you?"

"I don't know," I whisper, feeling my eyes fill up, suddenly more afraid than ever.

"You need to talk to the police," she demands, handing

me a tissue from the front of her dress. "Have you told your parents yet?"

"It isn't that easy."

"Of course not." Another eye roll.

"No," I say, blotting my eyes with the tissue, "you don't understand. I'm talking to my father tonight."

"Well, if you don't, I will—and that's a promise. You have until eight tonight to spill it."

"Kimmie, I'm sorry."

"I know," she says, finally cutting me an inch of slack. "If it were up to me, all boys would come with a label: *Failure to take in small doses may result in irrational behavior, poor judgment, and estrangement from one's friends.*" And with that she turns on her heel and heads off to homeroom. The zigzag hem of her baby-doll dress flaps out behind her with posh precision, reminding me how truly talented she is.

And how completely out of the loop I've been.

46

$\mathcal{J}$ GOT CALLED INTO THE guidance office today. Ms. Beady acted as if it were just a routine check-in, but then she started probing—asking me if everything was okay, if I had a boyfriend, if I felt safe here at school.

I didn't give her an inch, even though a part of me wanted to. A part of me wanted to unload everything, just to get it off my shoulders.

Word is Ben came to school today. But no sooner did he step off his bike than a bunch of boys jumped him. It's all very vague as to whom the culprits were, but apparently he ended up with his lip split open and a bruise under his eye. The administration called his aunt and had him sent home for the day, but they honestly don't seem too concerned about his welfare. Their main concern right now is poor Debbie.

And poor me.

Teachers I never even had in class, kids I never even talk to—all have gone out of their way to offer a listening ear. And so all throughout the day, with each second look in my direction and every word of warning, I can't help wondering if I'm being like one of those ditzy girls you see in horror flicks—the girl who keeps tripping over her own stiletto heels as she flees from her perpetrator.

But I'm not like that. I'm going with my gut—with the tiny voice inside me, telling me to trust Ben, to hear him out, and that letting the school in on what's happening now will only get him taken away, when what I need right now is to talk to him.

It's after school, and I'm standing across the street from his house, having just walked from the bus stop down the road.

His bike is parked in the driveway. I cross the street to have a look at it, searching for any scratches, dents, or chipped paint—anything that might indicate whether or not he was in an accident last night. But, aside from a six-inch scratch on the gas tank, the bike appears perfectly fine.

A moment later I hear a creaking noise coming from next door. I peer in that direction. There's an elderly woman looking down at me from her porch swing. When she sees I've spotted her, she stops swinging—the whining of the hinges ceases—but still, she continues to stare.

"Finding everything okay?" a voice says from just behind me.

I startle and whirl around.

Ben is there. His lip is puffed out, a trace of blood lingers in the corner of his mouth, and the area under his eye is a dark shade of purple.

"What are you doing here?" he asks, his face completely solemn.

"I wanted to see you." I take a step closer to inspect his wounds. There's also a crescent-shaped cut on his chin. "Are you okay? I heard about what happened."

"Which part—the fight, or the fact that I'm the one who supposedly put Debbie Marcus in a coma?"

I glance over my shoulder. The woman is still on her porch, still looking in this direction.

"Don't worry about her," he says, motioning toward the woman. "People have been watching me and calling the house all day."

"What people?"

"Reporters, angry parents, people on the school board, people who don't even know me . . ."

"And the police?" I ask, remembering what Matt said.

He nods. "It's like what happened with Julie all over again—except this time I didn't do anything."

"This time?"

He nods again, but he doesn't address it. "I don't need this crap. My aunt doesn't need it, either. The principal called and told her I should take a few weeks off."

"They can't do that."

"It doesn't matter. It's done."

"And so what can I do?"

"Tell me why you're here?"

"I wanted to see you," I repeat.

"Which is why you were inspecting my bike?"

My heart tightens, and a lump forms in my throat. I look back at his bike, at the scratch on the gas tank.

"Is there a problem?" he asks, like he already knows the answer.

"I just noticed the scratch," I say, gesturing to it.

"And where do you think I got it?"

"I don't know. Where *did* you get it?"

"You don't trust me, do you?" But it's more of a statement than a question.

"I just have some questions," I say, to clarify things. "I mean, they say Debbie was hit around one thirty or two, on Columbus. That's right near my house. That's right around the time you dropped me off."

"But I didn't hit her," he assures me.

"Were you on Columbus?"

"What if I said yes?"

"That's not an answer."

"What answer do you want?"

"The truth," I insist. "Just tell me the truth, and make me understand. Debbie seems to think it was you—at least that's what she told the police."

"She said my name," Ben says, correcting me. "And she said a motorcycle hit her. But she didn't say I was the one who was driving that motorcycle." He stares at me for my response—like what he's saying is supposed to make things right.

But it's actually making things worse.

I glance back at the motorcycle, wondering if the scratch was there before, fearing I would have noticed if it had been.

"I got the scratch today," he says. "Some kids kicked my bike over."

"Really?"

"Is it so hard to believe?" He motions to his banged-up face. "So, what now?" he asks.

"I don't know."

He reaches out to take my hand. "I still need to help you."

I hesitate, looking down at his palm, not ready for him to touch me yet—and to know what I'm thinking.

But he takes my hand anyway.

His fingers close around mine. It's tender at first, almost comforting, but then he starts to squeeze.

"Ben," I plead, trying to pull away.

He draws me closer. His other hand cinches my wrist.

"Let go," I say, louder this time.

But it's like he doesn't even hear me. His eyes are wild. His mouth is a straight, tense line. He grips harder, causing my joints to ache. My body turns cold. My head starts to spin.

Ben's face is pale and furious—no doubt from what he's sensing. I look up again at the woman on the porch. She gets up from her swing and hurries inside. Maybe she's going to call for help.

After several moments of more pleading and pulling, I jab the wooden heel of my shoe into his shin. It catches him off guard, and I'm able to yank free. I take several steps back, all out of breath. A look of horror is frozen on my face—I can feel it there. "What just happened?" I ask.

Ben's trembling, too. He bites his lip, to stop the shaking maybe. "I lost control," he whispers.

"But I'm okay," I assure him.

"Maybe now, but what about next time? All it takes is one slipup."

"But there's no cliff here," I say, trying to make light of it, even though my insides are completely rattled.

Ben shakes his head, like he doesn't want to hear anymore, like he can't even face me now. "You're right not to trust me."

"But I want to trust you. That's why I'm here. It's why I chose to come here instead of telling the police everything."

I reach out to take his hand, but Ben pulls away before I can even touch him.

"I need you," I continue. "I need you to help me figure everything out."

Still shaking his head, he turns away and goes back inside the house.

I<small>T'S JUST AFTER FOUR O'CLOCK</small>, and since I know my dad isn't home yet and Mom's not answering the phone, I decide to go to Knead.

Spencer's there. He's teaching a group from the senior center. There's a frail, pink-haired lady painting a giant, boob-shaped mug for her boyfriend—one in which you actually drink from the nipple. I can't decide what's weirder—the fact that an eighty-year-old woman is painting it, or that she's chosen a bright blue base color with red and white stripes for the accent, as if it were some celebration of America. Either way, it makes me laugh, which is exactly what I need right now.

I rub my wrist, still red from Ben's grip, and then unravel my clay car from its plastic covering, eager to get to work.

"I'm glad to see you still working at this," Spencer says, standing right in front of me now.

"I'm determined to get it right."

"I know how that feels. Sometimes my work keeps me up at night. I feel guilty just going to bed, sort of like I'm abandoning a friend in crisis."

I nod, anxious to see what becomes of my piece—to surrender myself to the power of touch, as ironic as that sounds.

Spencer lingers a moment, watching as I moisten the clay's surface with a sponge and then carve out an opening for a door. "I have a feeling this is going to be your most intriguing piece yet, or at least the one with the biggest pulse." He smiles.

I smile, too, continuing to work my fingers along the car's exterior. While he resumes his class, I create a bumper and fine-tune a tailpipe. Then I close my eyes and concentrate on the power of touch and where it can lead me. I smooth my fingers over the clay, making the passenger-side door of my car sculpture open wide. I spend several minutes adding a dent to the fender and a gash to the grill, and then I put a bunch of holes into the side for no other reason than that I feel they belong there.

More than two hours later, even after Spencer leaves and turns the CLOSED sign toward the street, I continue to work, conscious that time is running out and I need to get home. My dad will be looking for me. I start to put everything away, catching a glimpse of the pinecone sculpture Ben and I made together.

I start to pick it up, but the door chimes sound, startling me.

It's Matt.

"Hey," he says, all out of breath. "I had a feeling I'd find you here."

I look back toward the door, surprised Spencer didn't lock it on his way out. "Is something wrong?"

His face is pale and sweaty. "It's Ben," he says.

"What's Ben?"

"He had an accident. He dumped his bike."

"What do you mean?"

"I mean, the guy went ballistic and started drag racing me down by the lake. I didn't even want to, but he started tailing me, getting right up on my ass. He even put a dent in my door."

"Wait—*what*?"

"You need to come with me. You're the only one he'll listen to."

"Is he okay?"

Matt shakes his head and looks toward the door. His car is parked right outside, under the streetlamp.

Without further questions, I grab my jacket and lock the studio up behind me.

"Where is he now?" I ask, once we start driving.

Matt turns the radio up—some heavy metal song—and then takes a bunch of turns, leading us onto the main drag.

"*Where is he?*" I repeat, talking over the music.

"The hospital. The guy was racing me and got carried away. He flipped his bike and plowed into a tree."

"And you called an ambulance?"

"Yeah, I called them. He was banged up pretty bad."

"Why were you racing? Did you guys get into an argument or something?"

"The guy went ballistic," he repeats.

"Yeah, but *why*? I mean, there had to be a reason."

"Apparently not for him."

"But that doesn't make sense." I sigh. "That's not like him."

"Have you not seen his temper yet?"

Unwilling to answer, I glance out the window, watching as Matt takes another turn, pulling out onto the highway.

"What hospital is he at?" I ask, noticing how we keep getting further and further from the lake.

"Fairmont." He turns his radio up even louder.

"Why Fairmont?" I say, competing with the music.

Matt shrugs. "It's where the ambulance took him. The EMT guy said there are more people on staff there tonight."

I dig my nails into the palm of my hand, eager to get there and to see him. The speedometer climbs up well past eighty. Meanwhile, the heavy metal pours out of Matt's dual speakers, making me even more anxious.

Finally, Matt weaves over to the right lane and takes the Fairmont exit. A couple of minutes later, we reach the center of town and follow the first few hospital signs.

The town of Fairmont is even more desolate than I remember; which is why I almost never come here. Only a small grocery store, a pizza restaurant, and a gas station occupy an otherwise dark and narrow street. I spot another hospital sign, positioned under one of the few streetlamps. It directs us to the right.

But Matt takes a left.

"You missed the sign," I say, pointing back at it.

Matt turns down the music and tells me he knows a shortcut, but we end up at a stoplight—one that seems to take forever.

The inside of his car is cold and damp—and getting more uncomfortable by the minute.

"I think we should go back," I say.

Matt scratches nervously at his face and then adjusts his rearview mirror. The pinecone air freshener dangles with his gesture, forcing me to notice the toxic scent in the air—like bug spray. "I think we're lost," he mumbles, turning down a desolate road, and then another, until I'm completely turned around.

There's a sickly feeling raging in my stomach as we drive farther and farther from the center of town and deeper into a dark wooded area. I glance down noticing that the door handle is missing.

"Relax," Matt says, bringing his car to a stop at the end of a dead-end street. There's a trailer parked in the woods, like maybe we're on the fringes of a campsite. He cuts the engine and then turns to face me. A relieved smile crosses his face. "Are you scared?"

My jaw tenses. I feel my eye twitch. I try to nonchalantly run my hand over my jacket pocket and search for my cell phone. But Matt notices, snatches the phone away, and chucks it out the window.

"Now's no time for a phone call," he says, moving in closer.

"What are you doing?"

"Relax," he says again. "I just want to talk."

"You lied about Ben."

He nods and stares at me. His teal blue eyes are wide and intense. "I had to. You wouldn't have come with me otherwise. . . . Right?"

I look toward his door, noticing his handle's still there. "What do you want to talk about?" I say, trying to play along.

"Us," he whispers, taking my hand.

I resist the urge to snatch it away. Instead I lean in closer, wondering if I can grab his car keys from the ignition—if maybe I can use them to fight.

"I still care about you, you know." He rakes my palm with his fingertips.

"I care about you, too," I manage to say.

"No," he says, peeking up at me. "I mean, I *really* care about you. I wish we never broke up. Why did we?"

My mind reels, searching for the perfect answer. "We thought we were better as friends."

"No," he snaps. "That's what *you* thought. You said you didn't want a relationship, but it looks like you want one now—hanging all over Ben."

"I'm not interested in Ben," I lie.

"Then, why did you come with me? Why did you seem

so upset when I mentioned his name . . . when I mentioned his bike accident?"

I move my free hand down my leg, hoping to reach for the keys. Meanwhile Matt continues to scold me, telling me how tired he is of watching me flirt with other guys, that I have no consideration for anyone but myself, and that I'm such a selfish bitch.

"My dad's going to be looking for me," I say, suspecting it must be well after seven.

"Well, let him look for Ben." He smirks. "That's who everyone's going to blame when they can't find you."

"They'll find me," I whisper, feeling a knot form in my chest.

"It actually couldn't have worked out better," he continues. "Ben's shady past, your sickening attraction to him. . . ."

"Did you hurt Debbie?"

He shakes his head and moves even closer. His face is only inches away now. "I haven't been following Debbie," he whispers. "I've been following you." He runs his finger down my cheek, then strokes my chin. "We never did get to kiss much, did we?"

"A few times," I mutter, remembering the last time we went out. The night seemed more like an appointment with the dentist than an actual date. It was like pulling teeth to get him to talk that night. He wouldn't relax or open up, but he still tried to kiss me before we parted ways. I turned my head in the nick of time—just before his lips bumped the corner of my mouth.

Matt traces my bottom lip with his thumb, like he's about to try and kiss me again. "You're so beautiful, you know that?"

Keeping focused on the keys, I move closer and press my mouth against his. Matt closes his eyes to kiss me back. Meanwhile, I reach behind him and try to snatch the keys from the ignition. They wiggle out. And make a jingling sound. Matt notices and grabs my wrist, twists my arm behind my back, and pins it there.

"You're such a bitch!" he shouts.

"Please," I tell him. "I'm cold. Turn the heat on." I gesture toward the ignition.

Matt relaxes for just a moment, as if he might believe what I'm saying, but then he reaches into his console and grabs a set of handcuffs. He pulls my pinned hand from behind my back to try and put the cuff around it, but I'm able to thwack him with my other hand; my fingers just miss his eye. He recoils slightly but then rebounds, grabs both my wrists, and snaps the cuffs around them.

He opens his car door and starts to pull me out. I let out a scream and try to bite his hand, but he pushes me back against the car and then squeezes my neck.

"Shut up!" he shouts.

My throat burns. I hear myself sputter and choke. Finally, he lets go, muttering how next time I won't be so lucky.

It's pitch black outside. With the door still open, only the car's interior light shines over our immediate area.

Keeping a firm hold on the cuffs, Matt leads me to the

rear of his car. He pops the trunk and turns his back to fish inside. And so I kick him, hard, right in his upper thigh. Matt stumbles back, but tugs me with him, still holding on to the cuffs. I raise my arms and try to pull away. Tears stream from my eyes.

"Enough!" He swings and misses my face. I duck away just before he can hit me.

I try to kick him again, but Matt pulls me closer, and I almost lose my footing. He pins me against the side of his car with his knee and then smacks me in the jaw.

The canvas behind my eyes goes black. Stars spray out all around me, and my head begins to swirl.

48

"*Y*OU'RE STARTING TO COME AROUND," a voice whispers.

I open my eyes. Things are blurry for a second. And for one relief-filled moment I think that maybe what happened was a dream. But then I feel my jaw ache—a gnawing, singeing pain—where he hit me. And I realize that this isn't a dream at all. It's just that Round One is over.

And I've lost.

Now that the blur of colors is lifting, I'm able to see Matt. He sits cross-legged right in front of me. "How are you feeling?" he asks.

I try to swipe a strand of hair from in front of my eyes, only to find that my hands are still cuffed together, only they're behind my back now.

"Where are we?" I ask, looking around. It's dark except for a small lantern positioned between us. We're sitting on the floor of a tiny room. Aside from a TV tray in the corner, there's no furniture, no appliances, nothing mechanical, just a thin layer of carpet beneath us.

"Don't worry," he says. "We're in a safe place."

There's a stash of food and a bunch of bottled waters sitting on the TV tray, as if maybe he plans on my being here for a while.

"I think this will make you more at ease." He reaches into a paper bag, pulling out my stuffed polar bear—the one I couldn't find last night. "I want you to feel comfortable here," he says, dropping it onto my lap.

I tug my hands away from the wall, surprised when they move—that the cuffs aren't attached to the wall itself.

"I've given you a little slack," he says, reaching behind my back. He pulls forth a piece of jump rope—I can tell from the plastic handles. "I meant to bring real rope, but even with all my planning and lists I somehow forgot to buy it. Isn't that always the way?" he smirks.

I peer over my shoulder, able to see a metal loop sticking out of the wall, by the floor. He's attached the cuff chain to the loop with the jump rope. "I've given you a little wiggle room, but you won't be able to stand. I thought it was only fair, seeing as you'll be sleeping here."

"What?" I ask, feeling my insides tighten up.

Matt smiles in response, thoroughly enjoying this. Meanwhile, my skin ices over, and my forehead starts to sweat.

"And before you even think about attempting to untie the knot," he continues, "save yourself some aggravation, because I'm somewhat of an expert."

I look back at the webbing of knots. There have to be at least forty of them, each tangled over, through, and under the next.

"Impressive, wouldn't you say?" he asks.

I ignore him and continue to look around the room, noticing a narrow door behind him and a window to the right. The window has its shade down and there are curtains hanging at the sides. "What do you want?" I ask, meeting his eyes.

"You," he whispers. "I just want to be with you."

Keeping my shoulders steady, I try to wriggle free of the cuffs, but they're way too tight. "We're friends," I remind him. "You can be with me whenever you want."

"You know that's not true."

"It is," I say, trying to sound convincing, running my fingers over the knots. I try to pull at one of them, but it doesn't budge one bit.

Matt sweeps back the strand of hair that hangs in front of my eyes and then moves in closer.

"If you let me go, we can start over," I say. "We can even start dating again."

"Do you think I'm stupid?" he snaps. "Don't lie to me!"

My heart beats hard. My head starts to ache.

"You'll be happy here," he assures me. "I'll give you everything you want."

"I want to be let free."

"Not now."

"Then when?"

"When you can say you love me and mean it." He moves the lantern to the side so he can scoot in closer. He smells like the inside of his car—that thick, poisonous scent.

Hot, bubbly tears work their way into my eyes, until I can't see. "It doesn't have to be like this," I whisper.

"Deep down, you wanted this," he says; this is followed by a kiss on my lower lip. "You asked for it. And I aim to please."

"No," I insist, drawing my face away.

"Yes," he says, moving in even closer. "You asked for it with the way you flirt, and how you always want to be the center of attention, and your recent attraction to danger. I know that's why you're attracted to Ben. You want some adventure in your life. You like the idea of dating someone with a dark side. And so that's what I've given you."

I shake my head, trying not to lose it completely.

"I should think you'd be grateful," he says, continuing to kiss me. He makes an invisible line of kisses that travels from my mouth down to my neck and then back up again.

I try my best to play along, to hold back my tears by focusing on something—anything—else. I look over his shoulder in search of something sharp. Out of the corner of my eye, I think I see a knife sticking out from the pile of food.

"I have something to show you," he whispers into my ear, sending icy-cold chills straight down my back. He reaches into his bag and pulls out a folder full of photos.

They're pictures of me—at the beach, in front of my house, by the shopping mall, and at the bakery downtown.

"I just can't get enough," he whispers. "I'd look at these when you weren't around, reminding myself it was only a matter of time before I'd have the real thing."

"Please," I say, hearing my voice shake.

"Shhh," he hushes, kissing me. "Everything's going to be just fine. You'll see." He kisses me a couple more times and then sits back on his heels. "I hate to leave, but I have to go. People are going to be wondering about you."

"They probably already are," I say, hoping it makes him nervous.

"All the more reason to get back. We don't want anyone putting two and two together when they notice I'm not around, either. If you're the only one missing, everyone will assume Ben's the one who's responsible. Even if they can't prove it or find a link, he'll get so ridiculed he won't have a choice but to leave."

"And then what?" I ask. "When they can't prove it's him, they'll still keep looking."

"Hopefully by that time you'll realize what's good for you. We can say you ran away from home—that your parents weren't paying any attention to you and you wanted to get away."

"So, you don't intend to hurt me?"

"Not unless you do something stupid." He turns his back to me, starts sifting through the stash of food. "It was fun shopping for all your favorites. I've got yogurt-covered pretzels, corn chips, and granola bars."

"I'm not hungry."

"Are you sure? I can feed you something before I go."

I shake my head, keeping an eye on the knife. It sits underneath the bag of corn chips.

"You really should eat something," he says, "or have some water. I don't want you to get dehydrated." He twists the cap off a bottle, holds the spout to my lips, and watches my neck as I swallow.

"You're so beautiful," he repeats, wiping the dribble from my mouth. He brings the TV tray to my side and dumps a bunch of yogurt pretzels onto it. Then he fills a plastic bowl with water and sets that on the tray as well. "You should be able to eat and drink without too much of a problem. The lantern has fresh batteries, in case you were worried, so I don't expect it to go out. I'll be back just as soon as I can."

I nod and glance at the knife again. Matt notices and pulls it from beneath the bag of chips, runs it down the side of my face. "Dangerous enough for you?" he asks.

"I don't like danger."

"Sure you do. Deep down, it's what you crave." He holds the knife right below my jaw and presses it against my neck. "Sleep tight," he whispers.

My lower lip trembles. My eyes fill with fresh tears. Matt nibbles my lip to still the shaking and then gets up, stabbing the knife into the wood right above the door.

Finally, he leaves. I hear him lock the door from the outside. Meanwhile, I try my best to hold it together and to focus on the knife, but I can barely see through the blur of tears running down my face.

49

ALONE IN THE ROOM, I listen for a car engine, wondering if Matt parked right outside, but it's eerily quiet. The scent of a burning campfire lingers in the air from the moment when Matt opened the door, giving me hope.

Maybe someone's nearby.

When I suspect he's gotten far enough away, I go to work at the knots. I run my fingers over them, searching for one with a bit of give. Adrenaline courses through me as I twist the rope, trying to pull at any bump or gather.

After just a few minutes, my wrists start to ache. The metal of the cuffs cuts into my skin and makes my fingers tingle and go numb. Still, I continue to work, trying to figure out where the knotting begins and where it might end. But it all feels the same. And my wrists are stinging now.

I try to slip the cuffs off until my bones ache and I can feel cartilage move beneath my skin, but it isn't working, even when I scrunch my hands to make them as narrow as possible.

I scoot forward on my butt to see how much slack I actually have—it's about two full feet. I take a deep breath and pull with my wrists—so hard I think the bones might crack—seeing if I can yank the metal loop out of the wall completely.

But it won't budge, either.

Breathing hard, I tug some more, until I hear myself cry out in frustration—a loud, high-pitched scream that tears out of my throat.

My legs flail. My forearms burn. Sobbing now, I let out several more screams, until drool drips out of my mouth and my throat is raw.

But still, nothing happens, and no one comes.

After a couple more minutes, I notice the room begin to darken and swirl. I glance toward the lantern, but it's still well lit. Meanwhile, my head continues to ache. Bile creeps up into my throat, filling my mouth. I lower my head, and the room spins even more, making it hard to distinguish the floor from the ceiling.

I close my eyes, but it doesn't help. My stomach lurches. A whirl of colors bleeds over my eyes, turning everything black.

The room closes in around me, and I feel my body soften and fold. I'm pretty sure my head hits the floor. I'm pretty sure the piercing shrill inside my ears is a side effect of what I'm feeling. The room blackens and boxes me up. And I feel myself fade.

50

*S*TILL SLUMPED OVER, I OPEN MY EYES and sit up. My arms are asleep. My head throbs. I try to whisper the word *hello*, but my throat is burning. And so are my wrists—a stinging, searing pain snakes down my fingers and crawls up my arms.

There's a spill of some sort beside me. At first I think it's a drink or some food, that I toppled something when I passed out. But then the smell hits me—an odor like sour milk—and I realize I've thrown up.

The bowl of water still sits beside me on the TV tray. Half of it has spilled out onto the rug and my jeans. Did I do that in my sleep? Is it from all my thrashing around? I lean toward it, thirsty for a drink, but suspicious that it's the water that got me sick in the first place.

What did he put in there? How long have I been passed out? What time is it now? I look up at the window, but the shade and curtains block out all light. I wonder if anyone's noticed I'm missing yet, and if they're on their way to save me.

My eyes fill up with tears again. I try my best to blink them away, to convince myself I'm going to get out of here. Glancing first at the knife still stuck above the door, I survey the room. It's actually not much bigger than a walk-in closet. I scoot forward so that my feet reach the side wall; then I kick against it, noticing that the interior walls are covered with fake paneling.

The room shakes with my kick. More water splashes out of the bowl on the TV tray. I kick harder, and there's more shaking, like the room doesn't have a solid foundation, as if maybe I'm not in a house, or even a building at all. I take a deep breath, remembering the trailer I saw in the woods earlier, wondering if that's where I am.

My pulse races. I continue to kick against the wall. The room bounces back and forth. And then I hear something outside—a screeching sound.

I strain to hear, and then I scream at the top of my lungs, until my voice breaks.

Still, no one comes. I can only hear the calling of birds outside now.

I close my eyes and kick harder, imagining the force of my blows actually toppling the walls over. But instead it's the knife that topples. It falls from above the door and lands in the center of the room.

Quickly, I reposition myself, scooting to the side and extending my legs. A cramp runs down my outer thigh. I do my best to breathe through it, to make my muscles relax. Meanwhile, the knife lies just beyond my foot.

I reach for it, but my leg cramp worsens, causing me to fall back. My shoulders ache. My left arm is numb.

I let out a breath and try a little harder. The handcuff squeezes against my bones, and I feel something snap. At the same moment, my leg muscles relax a bit, enabling me to move forward just a little farther.

My foot grazes the knife, and I'm able to slide it toward me. I scoot back and sit up straight, dragging the knife toward my hands with my foot. After several attempts, I finally manage to wedge the blade under my shoe, just inches away from my cuffed wrists. My arm still numb, I try to cut through the knots but end up slashing my thumb with the blade. Blood trickles down over the rope, making it hard to see what I'm doing. Still, after several strokes against the knife, the rope is cut, and I'm free from the wall.

51

*T*HOUGH MY WRISTS ARE STILL CUFFED behind my back, I get up and stumble toward the door. Blood drips from my thumb, spilling onto the rug and making me queasy. I position my back against the door and try to turn the handle, but it won't budge.

My heart bounds up into my throat. Did he padlock the door from the outside? I look behind me, noticing a lock. I flip it open, hear a click, and reach for the handle once more. This time it moves beneath my grip—only I'm not the one turning it.

The door flies open, and Matt stands before me.

"Going somewhere?" he asks.

I let out a scream—as loud as I can manage, in spite of my dry and splintery throat. Matt pushes me, and I fall on my backside. I glance behind me to see if I can somehow reach the knife, but it's too far away.

Matt starts to shut the door, but before he can, I jam

my heel into his shin, as hard as I kicked the wall. He lets out a grunt and comes at me. Teeth clenched, he grabs me by the jaw.

"I'm sorry," I whisper, trying my best to soften my face.

Matt's breathing is labored. His chest heaves in and out, but after a few seconds he softens, too.

A cool breeze filters in through the door, which is still open a crack. It's daylight outside.

He takes a moment to look around, following the trail of blood to the knife by the wall. "I'm impressed," he says, moving to reach for it.

At the same moment I draw up my leg and kick him in the gut. Matt lets out a wail and stumbles back. His head knocks against the wall.

I get up and hurry through the door. Outside in the woods now, I see that I'm in the middle of a campsite. There are trailers scattered around, but it looks as though they've all been closed up for the season.

I run as fast as I can, maneuvering through the under-growth with my shoulders and legs. I can hear Matt somewhere behind me.

"Run all you want!" he shouts. "You'll never find your way out of here—not before I find you."

I scurry down a narrow path, hoping it eventually leads to the street. Panting now, I see a dark blue trailer in the distance with a car parked outside it. At the same moment, a long, pointed branch scratches at my face, drawing blood. I can feel my skin open up.

I hobble forward, the cramping sensation in my leg returning.

Finally, I get to the trailer. The car parked beside it is abandoned. It has no wheels, the grill is crushed, and there appear to be bullet holes in the side. It reminds me of my work-in-progress at the studio.

I crouch down behind it and try to catch my breath. After a few seconds, I venture to look out. Matt's nowhere in sight, and I can no longer hear him. My legs shaking, I manage to stand up again. I turn around to continue on toward the street.

But Matt's standing right in front of me. He smacks me across the face with the back of his hand—a stinging, biting pain—and then grabs my shoulders, shoves me again, and points the tip of the knife into my neck.

I try to bite his hand, but he jabs the knife deeper— until my teeth unclench.

He starts to drag me away. My legs flailing, I try to anchor myself, to kick his shins, but he still manages to bring me to the front of the blue trailer.

And that's where we find Ben.

He lunges at Matt, tearing me from his grip. I feel myself fall to the ground. Matt comes at Ben with the knife, but Ben is able to grab Matt's wrist, twist his arm back, and grab the knife right out of his hand. He throws it deep into the forest.

Matt barrels into him, but Ben pushes him away, and punches him in the jaw. Matt lets out a groan and stumbles back, but still he rebounds. He comes at him again.

Ben punches him once more—this time in the gut. Matt goes reeling backward, tripping over a rock. He lands on his back, hard, against a cluster of rocks.

Finally, he passes out. Police sirens sound in the distance.

"Are you okay?" Ben asks, making his way over to me. His expression is a mix of fear and fatigue.

I nod, and he grabs my forearm to help me up. Only he doesn't let go.

"Thank you," I whisper, on my feet now.

"You're welcome," he says. His lips curl into a slight smile, relieved maybe by what he's sensing—or what he's not sensing, more likely.

Maybe the danger is finally over.

52

I'T'S BEEN FIVE DAYS SINCE Matt's arrest and I'm off from school with the principal's permission. Word is he even called Ben's aunt to apologize personally for all the harassment Ben's had to endure, and to thank him for saving my life.

"I feel like such a shit for giving you a hard time about not being a good friend," Kimmie says.

She, Wes, and I are sharing a Peanut Butter Barrel at Brain Freeze.

"I mean, we knew you were in trouble, but who expected *that*?" she says. "Tied up and handcuffed—"

"And not willingly," Wes adds.

"Well, I'm done being out of the loop," I say. "From now on I want the full scoop on what's going on with you guys—every detail about your workshop at the Fashion Institute," I tell Kimmie, "and all the drama about both of your dads."

"I've hired a girlfriend," Wes says. "Her name is Wendy, she's eighteen years old, and I met her at the Pump & Munch. She filled my tank, checked my oil, and we got to talking."

"And why am I just hearing about this now?" Kimmie asks.

"She's pretty," he says, ignoring the question, "charges a reasonable hourly fee, and comes by my house once a week to hang on me, which makes my dad happy."

"Well, that sounds healthy," I tease.

"Say what you will, but I'm done talking on this subject." He takes a giant shovelful of ice cream to avoid answering any more questions.

"Okay, so, speaking of disturbing and dysfunctional," Kimmie continues, "my mom has finally caved to my dad's wacko ways. They're going to a body piercer Saturday night to celebrate their twentieth wedding anniversary."

Wes shivers in response, but I can't help letting out a giggle.

"Laugh now, but it won't be too funny when they're asking to borrow your sterling silver hoops to decorate their various body parts."

"Very true," I say, glancing down at my watch. Only ten minutes until Ben is supposed to meet me here. I haven't really spoken to him since Matt's arrest. It's not that I haven't wanted to. It's just that my mother's kept me on a pretty short leash ever since I went missing.

Needless to say, my parents completely freaked when I didn't come home that night or the following day.

Only, instead of breaking my mother down even more, it actually seemed to help put things into perspective for her.

"Maybe if I hadn't been so out of it," she said, sitting beside me on her meditation mat last night, "you could have confided in me. We could have avoided this whole situation."

"It's not your fault," I assured her. "I should have said something sooner."

My mother hugged me, promising she'd always be there for me, and that she's even decided to go visit Aunt Alexia at the hospital once and for all.

"So, what happens now with Stalker Boy?" Wes asks, his mouth full of peanut butter ice cream. "Community service with a slap or somebody's boy-bitch behind bars?"

"Maybe neither. It's still too soon to tell."

"I bet it'll be a whole lot worse for him if Debbie doesn't get better," Wes says.

I nod, knowing he's right. It turns out Debbie wasn't getting stalked at all, but her so-called friends thought it would be funny to make it look as though somebody was after her. They were the ones who left notes on her locker and put ideas in her head, totally messing with her mind. Apparently the same friends were responsible for a lot of the school's graffiti, including the mascot sign in the back parking lot. Debbie had gotten paranoid, completely convinced somebody was following her on a constant basis. Even though nobody was.

A witness came forward, saying he'd seen her walking home on the night of the accident. He said she'd kept looking over her shoulder, not really paying attention to where she was going. He'd even tried to get her attention, because she'd kept stumbling out onto the street. The guy had thought she was drunk, but there was nothing found in her system—just pure paranoia. In the end it was a car that hit her, not a motorcycle.

"Honestly," Kimmie says, "did you ever suspect that Matt was the one leaving those photos of you? I mean, whoever would have thought he could be such a psycho? See, I told you he was lying about dating Rena Maruso. A girl like me doesn't miss a scoop that scandalous."

I shrug, remembering my good times with Matt, sipping coffee and studying French at the Press & Grind, and then how malicious he got in the back of his parents' trailer, even drugging me with some tranquilizers he put into the water.

"So, where does this leave things with you and Mr. Benilicious?" Kimmie asks.

"Do I smell a role-playing game involving superhero costumes and lots of body butter?" Wes gives his shovel a good lick.

"Speaking of touchy-feely games," Kimmie says, "how hot is it that Ben was able to predict that Matt was the psycho in question by feeling up your sculpture?"

I smirk, thinking about the irony of it all—how I'd always spent so much time trying to control my work, to have it fit within the parameters of some self-created ideal, but how it was when I went with my gut and let my art control me, that something really great happened. Something palpable.

After I went missing, Ben went to Knead in search of my latest piece. Spencer pointed him in the direction of my car sculpture. Ben touched it, following the imprints of my fingers, still able to feel traces of me there.

After only a few minutes, he could sense that Matt was the one who was after me. And so he followed him, right to the trailer where I was being held. As soon as he got to the campsite, he knew for sure something wasn't right and dialed 911.

"I guess my sculpture has a pulse," I say.

"More than a pulse, honey," Kimmie says. "That piece must have a brain, breath, and heartbeat."

"So, what do you think Ben wants to talk to you about?" Wes asks.

I shake my head and look away, not really knowing how things stand or if he even wants to talk to me at all. Aside from agreeing to meet with me today, now that I'm safe—that his work is done, maybe—he's been acting sort of distant.

"Well, I guess we'll all find out soon enough." Kimmie motions to the door.

Ben is standing there. He looks even more amazing than usual—windblown hair, tanned skin, and a bit of scruff on his face, like he just woke up.

He waves, and I head over to join him.

"Hey," he says, smiling slightly.

"Hi." I smile back.

But then his smile fades, and he turns away, opens the door wide, and follows me out. We take a walk to the beach, just like last time, and sit on a bench that overlooks the water.

"It's so much easier to be here now," he says, finally. "I don't sit here hating myself for what happened to Julie."

"I'm glad," I say, angling myself toward him.

Ben finally looks at me. His expression is as solemn as it was just moments ago at the door. "I'm not going back to school."

"What do you mean?"

"I mean, I'm going to take some time off for a bit—go back to the whole homeschooling routine, but with real tutors this time. Maybe I'll even travel somewhere. I have a cousin in Boston who's been asking me to visit for a while."

"You can't quit school."

"I'm not quitting. I just need a break. It's been an intense couple of weeks."

"When will you be back?"

"I'm not sure. Principal Snell's given me permission to come back for second term, as long as I keep up with all my work."

"And so, what about us?"

Ben looks back at the ocean. The scar on his arm is completely visible now, like he no longer feels the need to hide it. "We should probably take a break, too."

"What if I don't want to take a break?"

"You're not going to make this easy, are you?"

I shake my head. "I don't understand. I mean, things were just getting good."

"For me, too."

"Then, stay."

"I know it doesn't make sense," he sighs, "but I'm doing this for you."

"I don't want you to."

"Maybe not now."

"Maybe not *ever*."

"And maybe in time you'll see it's for the best."

I let out a breath, unwilling to accept what he's saying, feeling my eyes turn to liquid. "Why?" I ask. My voice quavers.

"It's hard to explain," he says, looking back at me now. "But remember that look you gave me when I touched you that last time, when I squeezed you too hard? It reminded me of Julie—of how scared she was, too."

"I know you didn't mean to hurt me."

"You're right." He nods. "I *didn't*. But even after I snapped out of it, I could still see the mistrust in your eyes."

"I trust you now," I assure him.

"But that's just it; maybe you shouldn't. Maybe somebody like me can't ever be fully trusted."

"Don't talk like that." I wipe my eyes with my sleeve.

"You're safe," he says, his eyes filling up now, too. "Let's keep it that way."

"You won't hurt me. I want to be with you."

"Maybe someday," he says, leaning in closer. His forehead grazes mine, making me eager for more.

There's a crumbling sensation inside my chest. Tears drip down the sides of my face. "Don't go. I need you."

"You *don't* need me. You have good survival instincts, remember?"

"Don't go," I repeat, louder this time. I pull him in closer, so that his heart pounds against my chest.

"Stop," he whispers, but he wraps his arms around my waist.

I run my fingers down his back and breathe into his neck.

"This isn't easy for me." His fingers tremble against my skin, right below the hem of my sweater, as if he's trying his best to control himself.

"Please," I insist, kissing his cheek. He tastes like sugar and salt.

He draws me closer. His fingers knead my skin— almost a little too hard. There's heat coming from his touch.

He pulls away, all out of breath. His eyes are red and watery. "I'm sorry." He motions to my waist, where his fingers have left a mark.

"I'm fine," I assure him, pulling my sweater down.

He gets up and lingers a moment, just looking at me, as if maybe a part of him doesn't want to leave.

But then he tells me good-bye anyway.

Acknowledgments

I'm so grateful to have such talented and supportive people in my corner. A huge thank-you to my amazing agent, Kathryn Green, for her literary and professional advice, and to my editor, Jennifer Besser, for her thoughtful comments, invaluable suggestions, and endless supply of enthusiasm.

Thanks to my biggest fans: Ed, Ryan, Shawn, and Mom. You've been there for me page by page, offering support, time to write, and a sense of humor whenever I need it. I'm so lucky.

A special thanks to Don Welch, Computer Expert Extraordinaire, who helped retrieve *Deadly Little Secret* when my computer had plans of its own. I bow to your technical greatness.

I'm lucky to have the support and encouragement of friends, family members, and fellow young adult authors with whom I can talk shop. You know who you are; thank you so much for being there.

And lastly, colossal, humongous, and gargantuan thanks go to my readers. I know I say this all the time, but I'm so truly grateful for every letter, every e-mail, each book trailer, art project, book-inspired school assignment, fan blog, and other correspondence you send my way and/or create for my books. You guys are truly the very best!

Look for the next book
in the Touch series,
DEADLY LITTLE LIES

DEADLY LITTLE LIES

J'VE BEEN HAVING TROUBLE SLEEPING. Most nights, I find myself lying awake in bed, unable to nod off.

And unable to take my mind off him.

The strength of his hands.

The way he smelled—a mix of sugar and sweat.

And the branchlike scar that snaked up his arm.

Ever since Ben left four months ago, I've been getting fixated on these little things, trying to remember if his scar had three branches or four, if it was his left or his right thumb knuckle that always looked a little swollen, and if his sugary smell was more like powdered doughnuts or cotton candy.

Sometimes I think I'm going crazy. And I'm not just saying that to be dramatic. I really question my sanity. Things just haven't been right lately. *I* haven't been right.

And I guess that's what scares me the most.

Like last night. Once again unable to sleep, I crept into the hallway and down to the basement. My dad, who firmly believes that we all should have our own personal work space, has designated the area behind his tool bench as my pottery studio. And so I have a wheel, bins full of carving tools, and boxes of clay just waiting to be sculpted.

Wearing a nightshirt and slippers, I decided to work in the dark, inspired by the moon as it poured in through the window, slicing a long strip of light across my table. I cut myself a thick hunk of clay and began to knead it out. With my eyes closed I could feel the moonlight tugging at the ends of my hair, shining over my skin, and swallowing my hands whole.

Keeping focused on the clammy texture of the clay and not what I was actually forming, I tried to relax—to stop the whirring inside my mind.

But then it hit me. The image of Ben's scar popped into my head. And so I started sculpting it—feeding this weird, insatiable need inside me to form his arm, from his fingertips to just past his elbow. My fingers worked fast, as if independent of my mind—as if they knew exactly the way things should be, while my brain just couldn't keep up.

At least thirty minutes later, long after my fingers had turned waterlogged, I took a step back to take it all in— what I had sculpted and what it could possibly mean. Sitting on my worktable was my sculpture of Ben's arm— his scar, the muscles in his wrist, and the bones in his hands.

It was exactly the way it should be—exactly the way I remembered it.

His scar had three branches, not four.

It was his left thumb that looked a little bit swollen, not the right.

The answers to my obsessive little thoughts were right there. I'd sculpted them all out, which absolutely baffled me.